Copyright © 2020

The rights of Cheryl Elaine to be identified as the author of this work have been asserted in accordance with the Copyright, Designs and Patents Act 1988. All rights reserved.

Except for the quotation of small passages for the purposes of criticism and review, no part of this publication may be reproduced, stored in a retrieval system, or transmitted, in any form or by any means, electronic, mechanical, photocopying, recording or otherwise, except under the terms of the Copyright, Designs and Patents Act 1988, and without the prior consent of the publisher.

This book is a work of fiction and, except in the case of historical fact, any resemblance to actual persons, living or dead, is purely coincidental. A record of this book is available from the British Library.

ISBN 978-1-9996204-6-2

To Michael
Best wishes
Cheryl Elaine
(al

Dedicated to my book-loving family

For all the love and support, and for the wonderful friendships.
Reading really
does bring people together.

Camp Hell

Cheryl Elaine

Preface

I wondered if I had what it took to survive. Whether I could pick up my shattered body and crushed soul and piece them back together again. When one door opened another terrifying experience was forced upon me; I entered a place of horror and torment, a place where freedom and choices were stripped and I had no choice but to lay myself bare. Ground down, strength diminished, I was reduced to nothing. It was difficult playing to their command, dancing to their tune, yet, over time, I was moulded by their very hand.

Forced by brutality, I faced despair and an irreversible cruel action that no man, woman, or child should ever have to suffer. They had no empathy — chains are binding. Sometimes, invisible scars run deep, though they're often on display for the world to see.

This is my story, my truth, my time to unlink the shackles that bound me to slavery.

Chapter One

Imprisoned

I couldn't outrun them. My chest heaved from exertion, and my legs felt weak and limp. My vision was distorted from the constant downpour. My hair was drenched, and my body trembled. What did they want from me? I had nothing to give. I'd lived on the streets for some time— homeless, begging for spare change. I had nothing to offer. Was my suffering not enough? All I owned were the clothes on my back and the trainers on my feet. I'd heard whispers on the streets that others had been mugged for their clothes; no way were those two strangers taking mine.

Determined, I picked up my pace, even though my body hurt. I skirted round a corner, panting for breath, only to find a dead end. Panic surged through every nerve ending. There was no escape. My mind screamed with fear. My heart thrummed, like it was ready to combust. Although all was quiet except for the whipping wind, I could not see a single soul who could help me. I searched frantically in the darkness for an exit…maybe there was a drain to clamber into, with the rats and the eight-legged freaks. The reality was far more sinister than any fantasy escape. It was no use. I had nowhere to hide, and the looming truth was…I had no means to break free.

Cornered, with a concrete wall against my back and with nowhere to scuttle, I became a timid mouse, trapped by alley cats. I was petrified. My whole body shook violently; my thoughts prevented me from being still. I fixed my gaze on the harrowing shadows that were closing in, the stomping of their boots on the ground growing in volume. One guy was short and stocky—the other, lanky. Hoodies masked their faces.

I pressed my back tighter to the wall, frozen with cold fear and quickening despair. Rushed thoughts surged to the forefront of my mind—it was time to die, in the rain, in the dirt, all alone. Their footsteps grew closer. Muffled voices and echoing laughter came, then the impact of a clenched fist that flew with great force and sped through the air.

The man's knuckles struck me hard, and a surge of pain hit me with impact, a hammer flattening dough. A scream escaped my lips and rang in my ears. All my strength seemed to evaporate, and my limbs turned to jelly. Flashes of light blinded me as pain ricocheted through my skull. I struggled to see and eventually succumbed to blackness.

Sometime later, my eyelids were heavy, like steel weights dragging at the skin . I struggled to open my eyes. Every feature on my face stung, as though I'd been slapped with a sledgehammer. A constant pain throbbed. The impact of the man's fist on my face had left an ugly mark, and I had a lump on the back of my skull that throbbed violently where my head had bounced off the wall. A stench lingered in the air; I brought up my hands to barricade my nose and block the rotten smell. It was of something rotting, something unsanitary—even my nostrils grimaced at the putrid aroma.

Where the hell was I? Fear prompted me to sit upright; quickly, I scanned my whereabouts, taking in every detail of the compact area. I didn't recognise my surroundings at all. The situation didn't look good. Spots of black mould grew vigorously up the walls, and a hoard of old takeaway cartons had been discarded, each one harbouring their own ecosystems. It suddenly occurred to me that I was in an old caravan. A run-down caravan, no more than a lump of scrap metal.

Panic-stricken, I was consumed with dread and stared into the unknown with unease. Every emotion flooded my mind. I was scared. I rubbed my pounding temples, trying to recall how I'd got there. Had I been carried or transported in a car? One thing was certain, I hadn't walked there. The most sinister question that took shape in my mind was: what the hell did they want from me? I'd been kidnapped, and whomever the two guys were, their intentions weren't good. After all, they'd assaulted me and tossed me inside the van, amongst the decaying filth. I'd been disposed of, like rubbish.

A wave of desperation washed over me. My thoughts swamped quick and fast. I explored every dark thought imaginable. I was afraid, terribly afraid. Maybe I was dead, and this was Hell. But the mist from my breath and my petite body shivering from the cold told me I was alive. I feared for my life…I had to escape, to run far away from there.

I massaged my temples to ease the thrumming pain and hoped it would summon a clue to my location. The last thing I could remember was the force of a fist as it sank into my face, then nothing at all. Obviously, I'd been knocked out. Kidnapped, but by whom? The same questions kept circulating, questions I didn't want to face. What did they want from me? Who were they? Gang members? Or worse, paedophiles? Where were they now? I mulled through my memory; my head buzzed as though it was filled with a thousand frenzied bees. Horrific thoughts flickered, but with little detail. Nothing seemed to add up. How long had I been there? How long had I been unconscious? How was I going to get out?

My nerves were upon me. I shuffled across the dirt and decay that covered the floor. I headed towards a shaft of light coming through a broken blind at the window. What lay beyond that window, I didn't know. My body trembled, but my curiosity and yearning for an escape prompted me to move. My thoughts ran amok. What if those two guys were on guard outside? What if they held me prisoner forever? Slowly, I dragged myself to my feet. I crept to the window and peeled back the corner of the broken blind. I held my breath, and my heart skipped a beat; I realised events were far more sinister than I could have dreamt. I was surrounded by numerous caravans, yet I could tell I was in no holiday park. There were hordes of Transit vans, each displaying mobile numbers for building work. The campsite looked a crowded mess. Several chickens and dogs roamed freely. A woman, bare-footed, with long, black wavy hair and a medium build walked past the window. Gold hung around her neck and wrists; her appearance was distinctive. The site was a gypsy camp.

Bile rose to the back of my throat; I couldn't stop myself from panicking. Anxiety coursed through me, as fast as a runaway train on a broken track. I hyperventilated, my stomach churned and crashed in desperation. Fear oozed from my every pore, and I was drenched in a cold sweat. A shiver ran the length of my spine. I was numb, not just from the freezing temperature that my body was struggling to endure, due to my drenched clothes, but also from the forbidding ice-cold, harsh reality. I'd been imprisoned, taken by force against my will—abducted by gypsies. There was no getting out. I was trapped. I huddled in a corner, surrounded by rubbish. Distraught and petrified, I sobbed until my cheeks stung.

Chapter Two

Family Ties

Brothers Steven and David Murphy were top dogs in the pecking order. Their late father had been the Gypsy King. Steve was the eldest of five, and he'd inherited the title the day his father passed. With the title came responsibility. Rules that had to be enforced. With the help of his brother, enforcing was exactly what happened. Yet, with any position, there were risks. Steve had become a recognised face between the Romani and the Gadje (non-Romani). Different cultural beliefs, family feuds, and pecking orders required a firm hand to maintain order. The Gypsy King had taught both his sons the privilege of gypsy blood. He'd passed down his problem-solving skills, which involved invoking fear in others and bare-knuckle fighting. Defending the family name and knowing your place was imperative to survival within the clans. There were rules, which probably contravened most people's beliefs. This particular group of travellers had a lifestyle that wasn't for everyone. They were proud to live like nomads; in fact, their way of life was seen as a blessing for the men in their midst, though largely primitive for the women.

Steve's daughter, Lavonia, was fifteen and coming of age within her community. She walked around the campsite aimlessly in skinny jeans and a bright-orange cropped top, which showed off her tanned skin and petite body. Her hair hung down to her waist, and huge gold hoops swung in her ears. She tried to forget the stinging coming from her reddened cheeks; her mother often chastised Lavonia with her hand as well as her vile mouth. That morning, she'd seen something on TV and asked her mother about school—she wanted to learn how to read and write.

Her mother had erupted instantly. 'Don't let your daddy hear you talking about such things,' she spat. 'Education isn't for the likes of us.' She further showed her disapproval with a heavy slap to her daughter's face.

Lavonia cradled and nursed her sore cheek. There wasn't any point snapping back, but her mother couldn't stop her mind from wandering. Lavonia's thoughts were of freedom. She craved it, as did her three younger brothers. Life wasn't fair. All she'd heard of late was her father preaching about customs. She had no choice, he'd informed her, she would marry her cousin, Lee, to preserve their strong gypsy culture and family ties. He sounded like a record stuck on repeat. Lavonia had rolled her eyes, though she hadn't dared protest, it wasn't worth the punishment. Her life skills had been sculptured by her parents' ways and beliefs. Though she yearned for something different, she had to face facts: education wasn't an option. She longed to put ink to paper or to paint on canvas. She'd often draw her finger through the dirt to form pictures. Something niggled inside, a constant reminder that this wasn't the life for her.

Her stomach twisted in knots; she didn't want an arranged marriage—she didn't want any marriage, truth be told—especially to her cousin. Lee was a total prick, and you could count his teeth on one hand. Often, she asked herself the same question…was it so wrong to want something more? She despised her brothers, they had a freedom bestowed upon them just because they'd been born male. She was sick of hearing the same thing: a girl's place is to obey both parents and husband, and not bring shame upon the family name.

Thoughts of fleeing often crossed Lavonia's mind, she'd even mapped out an escape route while her parents slept. Once reality set in, though, she knew it had been a dumb plan. She wouldn't get far. Her father and Uncle Dave knew everyone far and wide. The shame would mean a heavy hand for her mother to bear—she'd feel the sting of her father's fists, and she'd be shunned by the rest of the community. Lavonia had witnessed some wicked goings-on throughout most of her life, but since her father had taken over from her grandfather after his passing, things had become far more sinister.

Turning a blind eye was expected, her voice or opinions didn't matter. The community wouldn't interfere in any way, shape, or form when it came to the Gypsy King's business; any dabbling would bring forth serious repercussions. From a young age, Lavonia and the whole travelling community were taught several things: to keep their mouths tightly shut and their eyes blinkered to matters that didn't concern them. Calling the police on one of your own broke the forbidden rule—a rule not often spoken of, yet many had witnessed its severity, especially of late. Many were afraid to speak out for fear of enforcement, which carried severe punishment. Those who broke the rules were shunned, banished, disowned by their families, and their punishment sometimes resulted in death.

Of late, Lavonia couldn't stomach what she'd witnessed of her father. As a child, she'd blindly accepted the setup, but as she'd grown older, she'd questioned aspects of their way of life. Did curiosity actually kill the cat? Possibly, but recently she'd seen such hideous cruelty. The comings and goings of strangers of all races, both male and female; some old and others in their teens. Something was amiss. In the pit of her stomach, she knew these people weren't relatives or associates of the countless travelling families that lived on, or visited, the site. It was obvious they worked for her father. But what kind of work did they do? She wasn't silly, she'd seen these strangers often cowering before the Gypsy King. The regular beatings were hard to watch; afterwards, some people sported heavy bruising whilst others were never seen again. Lavonia considered whether these people owed her father a debt—and, if so, what was that debt?

Her mind wouldn't still; she hovered in the shadows, hidden behind an old oak tree, spying on her father and

Uncle Dave. Suddenly, her eyes widened and her jaw dropped with horror. What had that young girl done to receive such a beating? Who was this girl, what was her crime?

Lavonia felt sick, her guts twisted into knots at what she'd just seen. Every blow the young female suffered, Lavonia felt it, too. She wanted to close her eyes and pretend it wasn't happening, but she couldn't seem to tear herself away. Her heart pounded. She watched the young girl writhe in agony; her distressed moans rattled in Lavonia's ears. She wanted to yell at them both to stop, but she knew better. In one swift motion, her father picked up the girl and tossed her into trailer nine.

Lavonia sighed with a heavy heart; there were others, girls and boys, young and old, around the site, housed in various trailers. There was something about this girl that intrigued her. Maybe it was her high-pitched screams, or because they appeared to be of a similar age. Maybe it was because she recognised the fear in the girl's eyes.

Chapter Three

Big Trouble

Avoice in my head willed my actions. I had to get out of there, somehow, undetected. I became consumed by thoughts of escape. Through desperate sobs and with trembling fingers, I tried the latch on the door, several times. It was locked from the outside. Engulfed in despair, I couldn't find my voice to shout for help; I was also afraid of what would come next if I did...what lay beyond that bolted door.

It was no use. Instead, I cried until I could cry no more. I'd been a fool to run away from my latest carer, but life as an older teen in the care system had been unbearable. I'd been passed from home to home like an old deck of playing cards. I'd also overheard my social worker on the phone; they said I was in the 'too old to adopt' category, that I needed firm guidance—that I had underlying trauma and I wouldn't rid myself of my baggage. What she really meant to say was, I had underlying, deep-seated issues that meant I was trouble. What was the point? The care system sucked.

So, I'd run away. For three weeks I managed to survive the streets, begging for spare change. There wasn't a curfew, and I wasn't being passed around families just wanting easy money from the state, but who couldn't give a flying fuck about my wellbeing. I figured that the social worker was probably right—I was trouble. And now I'd got myself into a whole lot of trouble—BIG trouble—and I couldn't see any way out.

My thoughts were interrupted. My body stiffened, and I strained to hear. The sound of footsteps became louder, and the latch screeched across the metal frame of the caravan before the door creaked open. I scarpered on all fours and huddled in a corner, my hands around my knees. I couldn't handle another session of brutality to my already aching face. I strived to recognise the two men from the previous night; the hoods that hid their faces wouldn't allow it.

A voice with a strong, unfamiliar twang bellowed, 'Get in,' from behind the door.

I initially couldn't see who he was talking to. A scrawny man, in his late fifties, though he may have been older, was pushed with great force through the entrance. His clothes stained heavily with dirt and his boots clumped with mud. The door slammed shut, and the caravan shook then it was locked again. I considered that the scruffy stranger was a prisoner like me. He appeared tired, underweight, and distressed. He sat at the table and didn't even acknowledge me whilst gulping down a bottle of water. From his inside jacket pocket, he pulled out a tin foil package. He was eager to open it and ripped it apart frantically, wide-eyed. He chomped at the sandwich greedily, mimicking a starving wild animal, and then he eased off his boots, followed by his socks. His feet looked sore, and blood oozed from large blisters. His forehead twisted into a painful frown.

'Are you okay?' I asked shakily.

He turned his head towards me slowly. 'What do you think?' he snarled.

'I don't know what to think.' Tears escaped my swollen eyes.

'Save your tears, they don't work here,' he replied with a heavy sigh.

'Where is here?' I asked, sniffling.

'Camp Hell.'

A huge lump at the back of my throat seemed to take forever to swallow down. I couldn't stop the violent shakes that had taken over every inch of my body. My breathing became rapid, as though I was literally being suffocated by a blanket of doom.

Had my ears deceived me? 'Camp Hell? What the fuck?' I didn't want to believe it, but my heart raced as fast as the spinning wheels of a Formula One car, at high speed, and anxiety washed over me. I knew I'd heard the guy correctly, but I feared that if I accepted his words, this was truly happening. My instincts told me to jump to my feet, to flee, to get out of there as fast as my tiny legs would carry me, but I had no means of escape. The door was locked, and we were surrounded by a whole campsite of travellers. My chances were minimal to say the least. In that instant, I felt similarities to a flightless bird locked in a cage. Tremors erupted through my every limb, and petrifying thoughts circled in my mind, followed by more tears. I struggled to catch my breath.

'Look, you need to calm down.'

'Calm down? How can I? I'm scared.'

'Why don't you get off the floor and sit here?' He pointed to the seat at the opposite side of the table.

I followed his request. Maybe he could help me get out of this goddamn place? 'I'm Amber.' I wiped the snot from my nose, on my sleeve, and exhaled heavily. I tried to compose the upset and my breathing.

'John,' he replied whilst chewing on a crust.

'What do they want?'

'To work us until we break,' he stated.

'What kind of work?'

'For me, it's been farm work. Building and shovelling shit, mostly.'

'And for me?' I flexed my arm and revealed little muscle.

'I don't know, Amber. All I know is, I've been here thirteen years and I've seen young girls come and go.'

'Thirteen years! How? Why?' My mouth dropped open.

He shrugged and laid his head back to glare at the cobwebs that lined the tin roof.

'What about the police?' I said.

'What about them? They don't often come here, and even if they did, what could they do?'

'The girls who have come and gone,' I pressed, 'where did they go?'

'That, I couldn't tell you.'

'What can you tell me?'

He pondered for a moment and took a deep breath. 'That we're slaves.'

Chapter Four

Detective Crane

Few places depressed Detective Crane, but of late, Yorkshire had become the pit of deprivation. Every shop was a barber's or a takeaway. The aroma of Indian cuisine wafted through the air against a backdrop of boarded-up windows and charity shops. The city and surrounding towns stank of poverty, and graffiti told a story on every tunnel and wall. Crane had dreamt of becoming a copper since he was a lad, but his years in service had soon moved from shining ambition to tarnished ideals and simply plodding on.

Crane sighed heavily as he glared at the stack of paperwork piled high on his desk. There weren't enough hours in the day to tackle it, he thought, never mind the thousands of unanswered emails. His latest case was a runaway teen called Amber Hart. Documents confirmed she was under the ward of the care system. It wasn't his usual case—plenty of kids ran away from their foster homes and got hooked up with the wrong sort; however, there had been a sighting of her running away with a brief snapshot caught on CCTV.

He scrutinised the footage, frame by frame, searching for anything significant, but once Amber turned the corner on screen, she disappeared from view. He scratched his head, irritated that to his annoyance, the other cameras in the area were either out of service or offline. Goddamn local council was a joke. Who was she running from? Had she been part of a ten-pound-bag drug deal gone wrong or had a gang of troubled youths wanted a physical confrontation? The sad truth was, she wasn't the first teen or homeless person to go missing, off the radar, from that particular area, and he doubted she'd be the last. To his annoyance, there weren't any witnesses, and if there had been, no one would want to talk about it or get involved anyway; faith and respect in the police service had hit an all-time low.

Crane pushed his chair back, and its metal legs screeched across the laminate. He clasped his hands behind his head and stared out of the window, over the rat-infested town and towards the grey clouds that matched both his suit and his mood.

Crane wasn't your average cop. He was unethical. Over the years, he'd convinced himself that his actions had been justified, that he contributed his services and dedicated his time to fighting crime. He'd worked this job for many years, and often reminded himself that getting his hands dirty was the real way of policing—a way to get in with the lowlifes and the criminals of the underworld. That's how he got results. He caught the villain from time to time, but on other occasions, he became blinkered and his lips were sealed.

He had an anonymous source—maybe they could shed some light on the missing person's case. After all, the social worker had informed him, Amber Hart had lived rough for a few weeks—if he wanted results, he'd have to go to the streets and fraternise with petty criminals and pay with hard cash or hard drugs. As long as the source got a fix, information could be obtained. It was like dangling a lollipop in front of a baby, a crisp twenty-pound note would do the trick. A rat-eat-rat world.

His methods weren't always above board, but it wasn't really about pay-offs and raking in money. He battled his own demons deep down inside—pain, and an addiction he couldn't kick. His need for cocaine and punishment had turned stronger after the accident; he was never quite the same again.

The assault was more than thirteen months ago now. Crane had been on duty when he was ambushed by a group of teenage wannabe gangsters. He recalled it like it was yesterday. Several kicks to the head, resulting in a metal plate to his face, and multiple broken ribs. It wasn't about his injuries—broken bones can be repaired—it was the thing that couldn't be fixed: the shame. A video of the assault went viral on every social media platform for the entire world to see.

The images stayed with him…the teens laughing whilst sticking in the boot and chanting, 'Let's kick the pig senseless.' That was the day he'd hit rock bottom. The day his manhood became tarnished. Whispers from his colleagues and peers fuelled his humiliation. The video still circulated today, no matter how many times he tried to have it removed—there, in glorious Technicolour, for all eyes to see. He became that copper no one wanted to associate with, the butt of the joke. That was the day he lost respect—not just for himself, for the British criminal justice system. The youths got off. They were underage; they just received a slap on the wrist.

On the outside, Crane appeared healed; inside, he'd hit an all-time low. He'd become addicted to painkillers. He never quite faced this truth, nor spoke of it; he told the doctors what they wanted to hear. Eventually, though, his prescription ran out. He wouldn't be allowed back in service until he was declared medically fit, so he'd learned to self-medicate. Being in the force had its uses…it gave him access to an abundance of resourceful contacts. This network was on the wrong side of justice, but Crane needed help to fight his mental pain. His addiction grew, and it didn't stop there. Throughout his service he'd visited some seedy places, been mixed up with thugs, thieves, dealers, and lowlife criminals on a level that could be deemed unprofessional. The deeper he got, the darker his need, the more he became tangled up with dealers. This was followed by a reliance on backstreet whores— anything that would ease the pain. So far, the setup had worked; he was lucky he hadn't had a random drug test at work, that his senior officers hadn't suspected he was a cocaine user, but every now and then, someone had to fall.

Chapter Five

The Gentlemen's Club

As night fell, so did the temperature. With no heating or running water, the caravan was just a shell—a cold, damp, tin-can prison. I huddled under my jacket, the sleeves pulled over my hands. I lay in the foetal position on the dirty, makeshift mattress, cradling my arms around my body and rubbing myself for warmth. I was tired, but my mind wouldn't let me drop off. John had been asleep for some time; he snored loudly, his head slumped against his seat. The absence of light made it difficult to see, but my other senses remained on full alert. Muffled voices seeped in from behind the door. I willed my shaking body to still and tried to concentrate on what the voices were saying, but the whipping wind wouldn't allow me to.

The bolt slid across, the door was unlocked, and John stirred. I held my breath and focused on a beam of light—a torch on a mobile phone. A set of eyes came towards me. Maybe it was the police and I was being rescued. I soon figured that this wasn't the case, I'd seen that short, stocky silhouette before—the night I was abducted. Panic resurfaced, followed by erratic breaths, as one of the guys grabbed my arm and growled, 'Get up.'

For a moment, I was motionless, until his grip squeezed harder. I stood on shaky legs, petrified. John didn't say a word; he was awake, his snoring had ceased. I was dragged from the caravan and met with the sound of an engine. Before I knew it, I was thrown into the back of a Transit van, too frightened to make a sound or whimper.

The vehicle picked up speed and hit every pothole and grassy bump. I was tossed around like a leaf in a salad. Ten minutes later, and I guessed we were driving on the open road; the journey became smoother, although I held on to a crack in the metal frame for support. The two guys—who I later learned were the feared gypsy brothers, Steve and Dave—chatted above the noise of the radio; they were laughing, without a care in the world. I felt sick to my stomach. Where were they taking me? What would happen next?

Sometime later, we arrived at our destination. I was then led down an alleyway, wedged between stocky Steve and lanky Dave. They were talking about some tip they'd received on a fixed horse race. I couldn't help it, I interrupted them.

'Please let me go,' I pleaded, giving them my best puppy-dog eyes.

'Believe me, you're going to go all right,' one replied.

They both laughed. I sighed; I was the butt of their joke.

On the wall above the door, a sign in neon-red lights read Gentlemen's Club. I suddenly had a bad feeling and couldn't help but think, *For Christ's sake, I shouldn't be here!* Panic resurfaced, and my breathing became erratic.

I was forcefully ushered into a room full of scantily dressed girls. They sported thick makeup; some had heavy bruises, much like the ones that had appeared around my eyes. Oh my fucking God, I thought, as the realisation hit me like a sledgehammer to the head. Time seemed to stand still; everything was in slow motion except the beat of my racing heart.

A voice I didn't recognise repeated the same words over the hum of white noise. 'Put them on. Put them on,' said a woman in her forties. Her corset hugged her shapely curves, her bosom bulging at the seams; her stockings bore more holes than an antique pin cushion. She held a garment. She extended her arm, prompting me to take it. I reluctantly took the crumpled red dress then reached for the black stiletto heels, their straps dangling between her heavily bitten fingernails. Already, I could feel what was intended for me, as if sin itself was entwined in the dress's fabric. Bile rose at the back of my throat. I found it hard to swallow down and I shook my head in protest.

Lanky Dave stepped forward, invading my space. He wasn't happy that I hadn't complied and he raised his hand. My eyes flickered, and I flinched in anticipation.

Before he could take a swing at me, the woman with bulging bosoms stepped between us. 'You don't want to damage the goods. It's not great for business.'

'For God's sake, Jenny, always playing mother hen. Just sort the bitch out.'

Jenny guided me through a door and into a back room. Her features made her appear as cold as ice, yet she spoke softly. 'Hi, dear…' she began.

'It's Amber.'

Jenny rolled her eyes. 'Amber, your name's not that important. What is important is this…just keep your mouth shut and do what's asked, then it's easier for all of us.'

'I don't want to do this.' I held out the dress and heels to her, tears welling in my eyes as my body trembled.

'None of us do, hon, but if you don't, things will only get worse.'

'Worse, are you frigging kidding me? How can it be any worse?'

'Just trust me. I know.'

'Trust you? That's a fucking joke. I don't trust any of you. You're one of them.'

'Play it the hard way or heed my warning, it's your choice. But just put the goddamn dress on.'

I could tell that Jenny's patience was wearing thin. She obviously didn't want to feel the heavy hand of either brother. Hesitantly, she revealed hidden scars to me, the result of the last strike which she'd received for showing compassion towards the girls. It wasn't pretty.

Reluctantly, I undressed in a scantly lit room. I didn't have a choice. I pulled the flimsy red material over my head. The heels didn't fit; I tried forcing my size six feet into the size five shoes. I slid my trainers back on my feet.

Jenny gave me the once-over. 'No way,' she said, 'if the shoes don't fit, make them fit, we're not getting a punishment for you.'

I eventually managed to get the shoes on, and stood, my feet crippled. I resembled a backstreet whore. I fit the setting at least, but I wasn't comfortable. All I could think about was my virginity—I didn't want it taken by some dirty old pervert. Truth be told, I was petrified of what was to come.

Smoke filled the air, and a mass of male bodies lined the bar, a drink in one hand and a girl in the other. My stomach sank as quickly as an anchor drops to the bottom of the ocean bed. I couldn't move, rooted to the spot. *I can't do this!* Despair must surely be written on my face for all to see. Jenny gave me a reassuring tap on the shoulder. Was she a friend or foe? I caught sight of a dish filled with peanuts on the bar, and my stomach grumbled. How the hell could I think of food at a time like this?

The men were like vultures, and I had become the prize meat, whilst they eyed me up and down and frothed at the mouth. The mood felt predatory. I wasn't ready for the slaughter of grubby fingers on my flesh. As my anxiety escalated, palpitations took hold. The walls seemed to close in. I was light-headed, disorientated by the flashing disco lights and thrumming music. I put my head in my hands and wished the haziness away. A banging pain at my temples pulsated on repeat, unrelenting, a hammer constantly hitting a brick wall, and my mouth as dry as the Sahara Desert.

Jenny noticed my discomfort and handed me a glass of water. 'You do the bar tonight, it'll give you time to get your head round everything.'

I snatched the glass eagerly and drank it in one go.

'Now, for all our sakes, pull yourself together and grab a tray. There's money to be made.'

I guessed I should be thankful—I'd been given a better job than the rest, serving drinks, whilst the other girls danced, seductively, to the beat. I gave myself a shake. But I wasn't thankful, I couldn't actually believe my eyes. Men of all races, cultures, and ages ogled the girls' every movement, touching, groping, and drooling over underaged girls, sick paedophiles, the lot of them. I kept my mouth shut, but my eyes remained on high alert.

Maybe there was an exit. Well, unless I had the strength to battle a seven-foot-tall brick-shithouse of a bouncer, there wasn't. I hobbled, clumsily, with a tray in hand, my feet, as well as my soul, praying for release. The lights were now low and the music amplified. Some girls danced on poles, others on laps. Some went down a corridor and behind a red velvet curtain. I feared what was behind the velvet…at what lay in store for me. Horrific images raced through my mind. I needed another drink, something stronger than water.

I glanced round then quickly swiped a shot from the tray, followed by another, then another. The alcohol cooled my throat and calmed my nerves. More men arrived, and I found myself amongst a crowd of sweaty bodies, made up of punters and slaves. Being a waitress meant I was luckier than most.

The effects of the alcohol took over. I'd slugged back more than I could handle, partly to quench my thirst and also because I was hungry. I hadn't eaten for some time, since before I'd been kidnapped. Maybe I simply downed more shots to obliterate the stark reality that surrounded me.

I swayed on my heels; the alcohol took a hold of my actions. My stomach lurched, and the tray seemed to leap from my hand into the air. It crashed to the floor. Everyone stopped and glared at me. My legs felt like rubber bands, and beads of sweat formed on my brow. A force accumulated almost like a fire hydrant giving way to mounting pressure, and I was violently sick. Steve appeared from behind the red curtain. He scowled then grabbed my arm, and yanked me into the ladies' bathroom. I continually stumbled due to the ill-fitting heels.

My queasiness wouldn't subside. I held on to the walls of the cubicle until my entire stomach found its way into the toilet bowl. The room seemed to be moving. As I stood, I glanced at my clothes—there was vomit stained all down the front of the red dress. I was a mess.

'Stupid bitch! Clean yourself up,' Steve bellowed. He pulled my own clothes from a locker and threw them at me.

By the time I realised what was being launched into the air, they were on the filthy floor. I scuttled over to retrieve them and cradled the few possessions I had in this world. I could tell by Steve's face that I was in trouble. I was scared I'd get another punch to my face. The drink had scattered my emotions, and I suddenly found myself wanting to fight back.

I sniggered. I waved my finger in his face. 'What you going to do about it?'

A feral growl roared in his throat, and his eyes seemingly turned black. He reminded me of a soulless demon, ready to devour in one strike. I stepped back. He lunged forward, his fists clenched. He twisted my hair at the roots and tugged me closer, so his face was only inches from mine. His rasping breath stank of cigarettes. I'd overstepped the mark. What the hell was I thinking? The strength I'd had just moments ago faded in an instant. I quaked as he dragged me around the piss-stained floor, tossing me effortlessly as though I was as light as a ragdoll. I was helpless against his stocky stature and overcome with fear and panic. I sobbed uncontrollably. With his fingers still entwined in my hair, he hauled me up to the sinks. He jerked my head back, and our faces reflected in the mirror. One of us was a dribbling wreck, the other, a pure powerhouse of muscle.

'You see this?' He pointed at my reflection. 'She belongs to me.'

The fear of his punishment saw me motionless. At that moment, with my neck exposed, I was afraid he'd pull a knife and slit my throat. Maybe death would be better than his wicked intentions.

He thrust my hips forwards, pinning me tight to the basin. His body weight was against mine, and his stirring cock pressed on my back. I couldn't even scream. What was the point? Who would help? He grabbed the back of my dress with his free hand and, in one motion, ripped it wide open. I closed my eyes; I didn't want to see what was happening reflected in the mirror. I gripped the basin; my knuckles turned white.

'Open your eyes. I want you to watch as I break you.'

'Please don't,' I begged, 'I promise I'll do better.'

The door flew open, which stopped him in his tracks. I gasped with relief. Jenny burst in; she was breathless and waving her arms in the air.

'Steve, you've got to come now. Some guy wouldn't pay, said Marcia fell asleep on the job, and now it's all kicking off. The whole place is in uproar.'

Steve's features darkened even further. He appeared like he was about to combust. 'Goddamn that Marcia, druggy bitch! The fucking crackhead, I'll deal with her later.'

My eyes widened, and in that moment, I thanked God. A fight had preserved my virginity—for now, at least. My relief only lasted a few seconds, I was okay for now, but it didn't stop me worrying about further repercussions. Would Steve take up again from where he'd left off?

He disappeared from the bathroom at speed, yet I continued to hold on to the sink for stability until my body stopped trembling. I stared in the mirror and failed to recognise the naked girl with the swollen features. How had this happened to me?

Jenny let out a heavy sigh. She picked my clothes up off the floor and handed them to me. 'For God's sake, girl, why didn't you just keep your head down?'

'Thanks for saving me,' I whispered.

'Just get dressed,' she said and left me to it.

I quickly put my clothes on and ran into the corridor to catch up with her. She disappeared behind the red curtain. I approached the bar; it sounded like there was a riot. I turned the corner and ducked, narrowly dodging a stool that hurtled through the air. Raised voices and the sound of fists pounding on bones in every direction. The men seemed to be enjoying it; one guy was even taking bets on 'the pikey' who had a dark-haired bloke in a headlock on the alcohol-stained floor. Cheers came from all around me. The stale air smelled of ale and sweaty bodies. I wondered if this was my time to escape. I scanned my surroundings. Jenny and the other girls were out of view. I was scared to find out what lay beyond the red curtain; maybe that was where I needed to go. I was putting myself in harm's way, but it was equally as dangerous amongst the brawling hooligans.

I crept through the shadows, my head down. I didn't want to attract any unnecessary attention. I snuck behind the tussling crowd. I focused on the exit—it appeared bouncer-free. Clearly, they were somewhere amid the chaos. I peered over my right shoulder before descending the stairs. I took one step at a time, my heart pounding in sync with the beat of a steel drum. I met the cool breeze outside; freedom smelled good. My feet hit the bottom step, and a rush of adrenaline winged through me. Smugly, I turned and flipped the bird towards the club then got ready to run like the clappers.

Streetlights were in view, and a police siren wailed in the distance. A cloud of smoke wafted from my left, and a cigarette butt flew through the air, inches away from my nose. Dave appeared from within the cloud of smoke, as though he was a villain stepping out of the mist in a horror movie. If looks could kill, I would have dropped there and then. He gave me a twisted grin, and in the blink of an eye, his hands gripped me firmly around my throat. He applied pressure, and I struggled to breathe.

His voice rang in my ears. 'Your carriage awaits, milady.'

My escape, thwarted. Forcefully, he steered my exhausted body into the back of the van we'd arrived in. I gasped for air once he released me from his grasp to slam the doors shut. Within minutes, another couple of girls from the club climbed into the back. They didn't speak, they seemed too afraid to do so; they sat on the metal floor of the Transit, defeated. I wanted to ask them a thousand questions, but I was drunk and terrified of what would happen if I opened my mouth.

Sometime later, there was a heavy knocking noise, and the engine kicked into gear. The vehicle now in motion, I not only felt the effects of the alcohol, but also a complete loss of hope.

Chapter Six

Jenny

Jenny stood on the porch of her trailer. She gazed at the night sky and smoked a cigarette, her eyes following the flashing lights of an aeroplane. She wished she could fly far away. She'd spent nine years merely existing, cooped up in a run-down trailer. She made no choices of her own. She felt like she was living a life sentence.

She recalled that cold November day like it was yesterday. The day her life had turned upside down. The day everything changed. It seemed all fun and games — or so she'd thought.

She sighed heavily. You've really gone and done it this time, she scolded herself.

Her deep-rooted memories often resurfaced. Her mind flashed back to the weekend where it had all begun. She'd chatted with a guy over the internet; he seemed to have a heart as big as a bin lid. Her neighbour, Linda, had met 'Big Kev' online and, after a whirlwind romance, they were wed. Jenny felt a little envious; jealousy and loneliness saw her follow her friend's lead. Plenty of Fish seemed a good place to start.

That goddamn site had a lot to answer for. She'd fallen hook, line, and sinker for someone, but the relationship had brought her to the depths of despair. All she'd craved, as a single mother to a six-year-old, was a companion, yet she'd got more than she'd bargained for. She recalled that one night of pleasure...of hitting the dance floor, swinging her hips in time with the music, having a great time. Drinks had flowed, the lights were low, and the chemistry between her and her newfound love was on fire.

Steve had pulled her close and whispered in her ear, 'Are we going back to your place?'

Jenny had laughed and nodded in agreement. It had been years since she'd felt a man's touch, and the thought excited her. They huddled close in the back of a taxi, hand in hand.

'I can't let the babysitter see you, or I'll end up the talk of the town,' she'd teased.

Steve had waited patiently in the shadows outside the block of flats. He saw a young girl, about seventeen, wave at

Jenny who was at her window. The girl got into a waiting car. Steve was thankful the sitter hadn't caught a glimpse of him; leaving no trace or means of identification was beneficial to his agenda. Unbeknown to Jenny, Steve's intentions were not sincere. His plan had been in motion from their first flurry of text messages. Desperate cow, he'd thought. Jenny had made his life so much easier; he'd needed her and her brat as leverage. But first, he wanted to try the goods and have his fill.

Jenny checked on her daughter, Olivia. She was tucked up, deep in slumber. Jenny's mind was full of romantic inclinations and a night of hot, steamy passion. Steve had already stripped; he crawled on top of her. She received no kisses or tenderness, much to her disappointment. It was more of an awkward fumble between them and an offloading on his part. Steve then fell asleep, snoring heavily.

The next morning, when Jenny woke, her instinct told her something wasn't right. Steve was nowhere to be seen, and her bedroom door was closed. The bedside clock said 12.05 p.m., which was odd. She sat upright, dehydrated, a little woozy, and blood rushed to her brain, scratching at her bed hair. She clearly remembered setting the alarm for 7.30 a.m.; she'd wanted to be up before her daughter—she didn't want Olivia to find her mum in bed with a stranger. She'd never slept in before. Maybe it was the aftereffects of the booze.

Jenny rubbed her throbbing temples. Where was Olivia? Why hadn't she come to wake her up? Steve hadn't left a number on the bedside cabinet—he'd probably done a disappearing act at the crack of dawn. How wrong could she have been? She quickly wrapped a dressing gown around her naked body.

'Olivia? Olivia, Mummy's here,' she called, desperate to make amends for leaving the child to fend for herself.

Jenny's head was full of promises to make up for her poor parenting skills—she'd give Olivia a little treat, a takeaway or a McDonald's. It wasn't her normal practice, but she knew she'd be forgiven.

The TV was on much louder than usual as she walked into the living room. She couldn't believe her eyes. 'Steve…what's going on?'

He was perched on the two-seater settee, looking rather smug, with another guy.

'And who the hell are you?' she directed at the lanky stranger. An awful feeling swam over her, and her mind jumped to a number of terrible conclusions. She ran to her daughter's bedroom. 'Olivia! Olivia…!' she bellowed in desperation, scrutinising every corner. She searched inside the wardrobe and under the bed, but Olivia was nowhere to be seen. A series of 'what-if…?' thoughts rushed through her mind, then a realisation hit her hard. She'd slept so heavily and for so long that she must have been drugged. Where had they taken Olivia? What did they want from her, from both of them? Unwanted images tormented her without mercy…had they raped her beautiful daughter? Was she dead?

Jenny's legs quaked and gave way. A screech of dread escaped her lungs, then she became angry. Obscenities spewed from her lips. She found her feet and sprinted to the kitchen. With a knife in her clenched hand, she pounced towards the duo, cutting the air with the blade. 'Where the fuck is my daughter, you motherfucking sick bastards?'

Steve grabbed her hand in a cobra-like strike and twisted her wrist until she had no choice but to release the knife. It clattered to her feet, and the lanky guy scooped it up.

'Don't worry, she's fine,' he said. 'We won't lay a finger on her golden locks as long as you do as you're told.'

And so it began. Jenny became a pawn, forced into their evil schemes of brutality. Their rules were simple, but they couldn't be broken. From that day on, she was ordered to play 'mother' to a group of female abductees. Her duties involved readying the slaves for profit. Her payment was a meeting with Olivia every fourth Wednesday, though her ultimate reward was that her daughter wouldn't be touched, sexually.

Chapter Seven

Pain

Crane's anonymous source scuttled away down a back alley. He was already on the phone to his dealer, money in his pocket, arranging his next fix. The detective looked over his shoulder then he sniffed the white substance from his fisted hand and wiped his nose with a tissue. He wasn't sure if the information his source had shared was accurate; he'd heard that a gang of gypsies had taken over the area's drug distribution and was causing a bit of a stir in the city and surrounding towns. He warned Crane that they weren't to be messed with. Crane sighed; it wasn't much, but at least it was a start.

He jumped into his Audi and lay back against the headrest for a few moments, waiting for the effects of the cocaine to kick in so his body would feel as numb as his gums. He glanced at the clock. He had an appointment at 7 p.m. Eventually, he pulled up in the car park of a block of flats on Stanfield Estate. Crane took out the little bag of white powder from his inside pocket and inhaled another dose. He climbed the stairs to the second floor.

The detective had been seeing Clara for about eight months. It wasn't a relationship based on love, it was a business arrangement based on need—a once-a-week appointment. As soon as he stepped inside the flat, Clara was already in her role. Her hips were wide, and her voluptuous breasts bulged from a black basque. She'd scraped her dark hair into a ponytail, which sharpened her features. Although she was in her fifties and heavy-set, she never broke a sweat. She held a crocodile-leather paddle embedded with silver studs. Crane's need was about control, that he could withstand the pain of each blow. Kissing or intercourse wasn't an option, but detachment was. His pain was rooted so deeply—through trauma, intensity, restraint—that with each blow he stiffened, falling into a state of calm. Once the punishment was over Crane felt at peace, at ease, relaxed. He buttoned his shirt and dropped some money on the coffee table.

He walked a few steps towards the exit, then paused in the hallway. 'Have you heard any gossip about a gypsy gang?'

'Not recently.'

'But you heard something, right?'

'Years ago,' she said. 'Rumours and whispers, mainly. Apparently, my neighbour down the corridor got mixed up with some gypsy fella.'

'What number does this neighbour live at?'

'She doesn't live there anymore. Word got round that she did a moonlight flit with her daughter, left all her belongings behind.'

'That's odd, leaving her personal possessions behind, especially when she had a kid. Have you got a name?'

'She was called…' Clara paused. '…Jackie. No, Jenny, maybe. Not sure of her surname. Why the interest?'

"Just curious, something I'm working on. It may be nothing.' He closed the door without a goodbye.

Chapter Eight

Another Beating

Eventually, the Transit arrived back at Camp Hell. I was glad to leave the club behind and I was aware that I'd been drunk and very foolish. I was ravenously hungry. Almost being raped and having a hand round my throat had sobered me up quicker than any hangover cure. I'd escaped Steve's brutality, for now, but I couldn't help worrying about what would come tomorrow. What the hell had I been thinking? I needed to keep my scatterbrain thoughts at bay. Escape wasn't an option; instead, I visualised a hot bacon sandwich with lashings of tomato sauce. Food featured in my every thought. Surely they would feed me soon, but then again, I wasn't a guest in the hospitality suite. It was entirely possible that they'd see me starve. My stomach grumbled loudly.

I watched the other girls, they were escorted to various trailers, then I clambered back into the caravan, my tin prison. It was empty; there was no sign of John. Dave followed me in, practically on my heels. It all happened so fast…his fists and boots didn't cease. Excruciating pain ripped through my body. I hit the floor and curled my aching, throbbing body into a ball to protect myself, but it was no use against his sheer strength and his soaring temper. My battered and bruised body screamed in agony with each strike of his boot. His fists beat me. I cowered.

'I'll tell you when to drink, eat, or take a shit, do you hear me?' he spat. 'Next time, just do as you're fucking told!' His words echoed off the tin walls, masking my distressed moans.

Through trembling lips, I murmured the only word I could articulate. 'Okay.'

'Do you fucking hear me?' His teeth were bared like a wild animal asserting its dominance.

'Yes,' I whimpered.

He left, without any regard as to the pain I was in. The door slammed shut, and I jumped at the noise. My tears ran cold and fast. I hugged myself tightly on the cold floor, my body broken, wailing in self-pity and through the horrific pain. My chest heaved, and my breathing became erratic; I was overcome with feelings of terror, desperation, an anguish that wouldn't leave. For Christ's sake, I thought, someone help me. I shouldn't be here. I cried at what I'd been forced to suffer, for my drug-addled mum, and for all the foster families who had ever shown me kindness. My tears stung ice-cold against my numb cheeks. All I could think about was death. Death would be better than this. A black cloud hovered over me and wouldn't leave.

I must have fallen asleep for a while, through mental and psychical exhaustion. I woke suddenly from a night terror in a cold sweat. I was confused and frightened that the torment wasn't a dream I could flee from; that, in fact, I was actually living it. I thought of nothing but escaping—but how? Maybe John would help, but he wasn't there. I didn't want to believe it, I didn't want to surrender to the truth…that I would spend the rest of my days cooped up in that shithole, playing the dutiful dog of some gypsy master. What other option did I have? I had to push aside the pain and find some sort of weapon to defend myself. I knew my strength was no match for the brothers—even with a weapon I'd be useless against their muscle. With aching limbs and a defeated body and soul, I drifted into darkness once again.

The beating left me exhausted on all levels; I was out cold for some time. When a rustling sounded, I opened my eyes. John sat at the little table. He looked ghastly, a shade of ghostly white; his sunken cheeks made his face gaunt. His lips were dry and cracked. Once again, he'd obtained a bottle of water and a sandwich wrapped in tin foil. I glared at him when he unwrapped the sandwich, as though he was unveiling hidden treasure. His body trembled; he appeared cold and worn out. I couldn't help it, I was starving; I couldn't pull my eyes away and watched his every bite. My taste buds yelled out, and I licked my lips, imagining how the sandwich tasted. My body ached with pain. I trembled from the cold and through dehydration...all I could think about was the grumbling of my empty stomach. The only sound was of John chewing and swallowing.

I shuffled my battered limbs into the seat opposite, a hand cradling my tender ribs. 'Please can I have a bite?' I whispered.

He focused on me, taking in my cuts and bruises, but he offered no words of comfort. He glanced back at the foil between his fingers before tearing the sandwich in half. 'You look a mess, like you've pissed someone off.'

I nodded, tears glistening.

'Well, this will be the first and last time I give you my food. Learn to keep your mouth shut, follow their instructions, and you'll get fed.'

I nodded again then grabbed the bread. It felt soft between my fingers. I ate it greedily, swallowing it in three bites.

'Drink this.' He handed me the bottle of water.

'Thank you.' My emotions were mixed. Happy tears fell because of John's kindness, but a wave of sadness crashed over me at the horror of the situation.

John laid back his head and closed his eyes. Instantly, in the clicking of a finger, he fell asleep. I realised he was a man of few words, yet I needed answers to the questions swirling around my head—mainly ones about getting out of there. I wondered if he'd ever tried. I accepted that he was exhausted and let him sleep.

It was hard to tell if I'd been at the camp for hours or days. My hunger grew, and so did the pounding of my heart when Steve entered the caravan.

'Amber, come on,' he growled, hitching his head to the side, prompting me to move.

John stirred but seemed uninterested. I stepped out of the dark and into the light, squinting, the bright sun hurting my eyes. I was ushered once again into the back of the Transit. This time, there were no other girls, just me. I sat on the dusty metal floor, surrounded by tree branch clippings. Music blasted over the rattle of the engine, and my bottom felt numb. Every battered limb ached, and my thoughts fleeted to what was in store for me next.

Chapter Nine

Willow Farm

Steve wasn't worried. He was Gypsy King to the travellers at Brenton Common and proud owner of Willow Farm. He often spread himself between the two locations. He boasted often about his empire, and that the lavish farmhouse was built on the broken backs of slaves, a fact he took great delight in, and which made his status untouchable. With his hands wrapped tightly around Ben's throat, he felt alive. His brother, Dave, cheered him on.

Lavonia felt sad. She was sick of witnessing her father's cruelty. Ben's scrawny frame and nervous disposition was no match for such a big man. Ben had been a farmhand on their property for some time; he was slow, mentally, but he didn't deserve the torment that often came his way. Truth be told, Ben was a human punchbag, mocked by many travellers as they passed through, the general butt of the joke. Lavonia knew better than to intervene. She'd seen her father's quick temper many times; she could hear her mother's screams at the hand of her husband, the man who should love her tenderly. It wasn't a surprise — many of the gypsy wives were on reins, so to speak. It was the gypsy way that women were seen and not heard. Their role in life was limited to tending to their men and raising their young. Lavonia often wondered why God had given her a tongue if she was never to use it.

She watched her father toss Ben in the air, and wondered why bullying, fighting, and cash were the most prominent things in his life. Cash was always on a traveller man's mind — who had the most, and how to obtain it. Deceit, lies, scams, and general profiteering at the cost of others was the main topic between the men. Her father's business had made a handsome profit — he'd purchased Willow Farm as a cash sale, by enforcing a lot of brutality. Quickly, the quirky farm cottage had become Lavonia's home, a permanent residence with mod cons, a huge step up from trailer life. Yet her mother often reminded her, 'You can never take the gypsy out of the gypsy, no matter where they lay their heads.' The whole family visited the campsite at Brenton regularly. Lavonia's grandmother, Eileen, Steve's mother, was a stubborn old bugger—she wouldn't leave the caravan site. She was set in the old ways; plus, she was able to keep an eye on the goings-on and report back to her favourite son.

Lavonia gasped at the cruelty she saw from the kitchen window of Willow Farm and shook her head in utter disgust. She grimaced at every blow her uncle and father laid on Ben. Ben was tossed from one side of the yard to the other, a human ping-pong ball, only there were no bats present. They thrashed him by hand back and forth, until his scrawny legs gave way. Blood trickled from his nose, staining his t-shirt. He sobbed uncontrollably while the duo laughed.

Lavonia wasn't sure of his crime. She wanted to yell, 'Stop it!' Instead, she sighed deeply and grumbled under her breath, 'I hate you for this, for what you do to him.'

She felt a bag of nerves, yet a fury accumulated inside her. There was nothing she could do, she was helpless.

'Come away from the window, its none of our business or concern,' her mother warned; she had crept, barefooted, behind her.

Lavonia jumped, startled by the intrusion. 'Christ's sake, Mum, you scared the bejesus out of me.' She didn't understand how her mother could dismiss their cruelty so easily.

Lavonia climbed the stairs. She stomped up each step with a thud in the hope her temper would simmer. Olivia carried a pile of ironing in her arms. They didn't speak, it wasn't allowed. Although Lavonia thought it a stupid rule, she knew not to upset the apple cart. She often felt sorry for Olivia, she always appeared so down in the dumps; her mouth was permanently a hard line, she looked dead behind the eyes, and her thoughts always wandered somewhere else.

Olivia was young and pretty, in her late teens, a little older than Lavonia. For as long as Lavonia could remember, Olivia had been part of the family setup. She cooked, cleaned, and had her own room. Lavonia thought of the time when Olivia had first joined them—she was young and always kept at arm's length. Her mother and father had sat Lavonia down and given her clear instructions from the start—Olivia was not there to talk to or play with. She was there to work. It was difficult growing up with someone who was practically the same age, but with whom any interaction was forbidden. Lavonia's brothers treated the girl like a dog...fetch this, clean this, make this, do that.

During the last week, Lavonia had noticed a turnaround in her mother's behaviour. She'd upped Olivia's workload, adding insult to injury with constant cruel comments. There was no point asking Olivia what was going on, she was a girl of few words—usually just a good morning, goodnight, and nods. Lavonia knew that disobeying her parents with any form of general chitchat would bring repercussions. Punishment had occurred occasionally; Lavonia had seen a belt lash Olivia's bare bottom until it bled. She'd heard her screams. It was better to mind her own business, let Olivia get on with her chores. It was better to remain blind—blind to the cruel, harsh reality in which Lavonia lived. She'd learned to keep her head down and her lips tightly sealed.

Chapter Ten

A New Destination

The journey seemed to take about an hour; it was hard to tell without a watch. The back doors of the Transit opened, and I was instantly glad of the fresh air. Surprisingly, I was handed a warm coffee in a polystyrene takeaway cup and a Mars bar. 'Thank you,' I breathed. I felt like a kid on their first visit to a sweet shop, but it wasn't long before I was locked away again inside the cold van. I wrapped my mottled fingers around the polystyrene, not wanting to spill a single drop. The heat of the coffee was welcome, and it soothed my icy hands. I gulped it down; the warm liquid quenched my parched throat. The chocolate bar tasted exquisite; I savoured every bite.

Sometime later, the vehicle stopped. There were no streetlights, and I didn't recognise the location, though it wasn't the Gentleman's Club. Even with the moonlight, it was hard to tell what time it was.

The blackness of the night sky surrounded the silhouette of a dense copse of trees. I shuffled forward, not wanting to venture further into the abyss, but I had little option otherwise. I was wedged tightly between Steve and Dave, who escorted me into an outbuilding. It was obvious they'd been here before as they didn't need a flashlight to guide them. My teeth chattered violently as the icy touch of the cold night air penetrated my body. There was something soft beneath my feet, and the stench of farm animals hung in my nostrils. The beating I'd received the previous day had left its mark in more ways than one; I didn't complain or whimper. I considered the worst—that the duo had brought me there to die. They could kill me and dispose of my body easily in the vast woodland. I considered how they would do it. Chainsaw? Knife? Strangulation? By feeding me to the pigs? Gruesome scenes from every horror movie I'd ever watched flashed before my eyes in an instant, much like a Polaroid picture.

My heart thumped so hard it hurt. It pounded in my ears, and I feared it may jump out of my chest. My eyes adjusted to the darkness, and I caught a glimpse of something in the corner. An animal, I presumed. I wished that humans were blessed with night vision; the thing moved around the shadows.

We approached. Steve flicked a switch on a generator. A single low-wattage bulb gave off a little light. I saw him for the first time–a guy huddled in the corner of the barn. He was heavily bruised and had a chain around his left ankle, shackled as though he was a wild dog. His head was shaved in an uneven mess. His eyes were wide, and his hands and face stained with dirt. He shivered, either from the cold or through fear—both, I suspected. I'd never seen anything as utterly devastating; his humanity had been stripped away in captivity. How could they do that to a living creature, did they not have feelings at all? They were not men, they were monsters. I felt as though they'd dragged me to the pits of Hell. My legs buckled beneath me. I reached out to stop myself from falling, but it was too late, my knees hit the ground, and laughter echoed in the air. The clinking sound of a chain rattled; before I could even try to resist, my ankle was cuffed like the feral male's. I wanted to shout, 'What the hell are you doing?', but my body wouldn't withstand another beating, so I kept quiet. Without any communication, Steve and Dave walked off into the distance. I held my breath until they were out of sight.

I turned to the wreck of a man. 'Are you okay?' I whispered.

He nodded. He seemed to accept the situation as normal. How long had he been there? What did the evil duo want with him? I also needed to find out what was in store for me.

'I'm Amber.'

The guy had a severe stutter, and he struggled to speak. Eventually, he managed to say, 'I'm Ben.' He smiled and brought his knees under his chest, resting his arms upon them.

I considered, what he had to be happy about? 'What is this place?'

'Home.'

'What do you mean?' I asked.

S-S-Steve…he looks after me. Gives me my d-dinner if I'm a good worker.'

I could tell by his speech impediment, his body language, and his constant blinking that Ben had a learning disability. My heart ached for him. 'How old are you, Ben?'

'Next week, it's my b-birthday. T-t-twenty-one.' He beamed.

I didn't want to burst his bubble and ask how the hell he could be excited about a birthday when he was a fucking prisoner, chained up in a barn in the middle of nowhere. I let him hold on to his happy thoughts and simply replied, 'Cool.'

I didn't sleep a wink. I wasn't thinking just of myself, but also of the vulnerable adult huddled close to me who had fallen asleep on my shoulder. He didn't seem to have a care in the world, or maybe his silence was for my benefit. One thing was for sure, this place wasn't a home—it was Hell.

Every sound added to my nervousness—eerie sounds, which I could only assume came from animals in the stables. The scuttling of wild mice and hoots from a barn owl. I kept my senses on high alert. The cold air had penetrated my clothes, and I felt damp, but I couldn't have slept even if I'd wanted to. Images of Steve and Dave, the barbaric duo, and thoughts of how they would kill me, swam in my mind. Hanging, cattle-prod, flogging…I considered them all. I guessed that the morning would bring forth my execution or whatever they had in mind for me next.

I watched daybreak through cracks in the timber, and my suspicions were confirmed. I was shackled in an old, run-down barn, which harboured its own kind of tiny monsters. I scratched at my skin; I was covered in insect bites. This wasn't living, it was barely existing. The conditions were horrendous. I wondered how long Ben had suffered there. We'd been tossed aside, left to wallow like pigs in our own filth. My emotions crackled with the ferocity of an electric storm.

Startled, I sat up on the dusty floor and tried to alleviate my stiffness. Sounds of movement came from outside the barn; something or someone was heading this way. My anxiety piqued, and I held my breath. Ben twitched; he became agitated by the noise and chewed frantically at his already-bleeding fingernails. Did he know what was going to happen? It was clear he was afraid, like me. The footsteps closed in. Every hair on my body stood upright. Only the dust mites stirred.

The screech of the barn door sent a shiver through my core. I squinted at the beams of brilliant light which burned my eyes. I raised my hand to my brow as a shield, but within the stream of light was darkness. Evil in human form—I'd recognise that stocky silhouette anywhere. It was Steve. My eyes welled up. Was this it? Was I about to take my final breath? Would it be the last time I saw the sun?

He stomped towards us both, dust kicking up beneath his boots. His every movement was intimidating. Steve towered above us then dropped to one knee to unlock the cuff on Ben's foot. I couldn't bring myself to look at him, I just kept my eyes low and my mouth firmly shut.

My heart raced.

He snarled, 'Ben, you're going to show this mouthy bitch the ropes.'

'Y-y-yes, Steve,' said Ben, nodding.

Steve turned his body towards me and grasped at my foot with his chubby fingers. He freed my ankle from the restraints of the shackle. I rubbed where the metal weight had cut into my delicate skin.

'Don't fuck up today,' he warned.

I didn't reply, I was too scared of the repercussions.

Steve appeared to like seeing me squirm. He snatched my face between his fingertips, squashing my cheeks firmly together, and pulled me towards him. His forehead scrunched into several hard lines, and he glared into my eyes. His breath warmed my skin. I quaked.

'I don't want to hear a fucking peep from you today, do you understand? No fuck-ups. Work or no food, all right?'

I cowered before him, my cheeks wedged between his vice-like fingers. I managed to squeak, 'Yes, I understand.'

Even though I dreaded what the day had in store for me, there appeared to be a glimmer of hope. By the sound of things, I wasn't going to be murdered or mutilated quite yet. Plus, the very mention of food was an incentive to keep my gob shut. I was literally starving, and my stomach grumbled in agreement. It was obvious that food was the reward for your tears, sweat, and hard labour. My mind visualised all the things I'd always taken for granted: a sizzling burger, dripping with fat; a pizza with all the trimmings and loads of gooey cheese.

'D-don't hurt her,' stammered Ben, his features screwed into a tight ball.

Steve eventually let me go. He laughed at my discomfort, his stomach bouncing up and down. 'Fancy her, do you, Ben?'

Ben's face flushed. 'No!'

'Y-y-you want to put your little dicky inside her, don't you?' Steve mocked.

Ben shook his head. 'N-n-no, I don't. Amber is p-p-pretty, though.' He glanced at me before turning back to Steve.

Steve slapped him on the shoulder. 'If you work hard, you might get a cake for your birthday—or a slice of her.'

I couldn't believe it. Steve was negotiating with my virginity against a bloody birthday cake, in exchange for a hard day's work. Surely Ben wouldn't do that, would he? Would he even get a choice in the matter?

As Steve left the barn, tears fell.

Ben noticed. 'Don't cry,' he said. 'Come and see Bessie.'

I walked a few steps behind him and out of the barn. Could this Bessie give me some answers, or even help me out of there? Would it be an opportunity to run?

To my disappointment, there wasn't a huge sign with Escape Here! in big letters outside. I was stuck in the middle of nowhere. Barbed-wire fencing surrounded the perimeter. We could have been in the Yorkshires Dales or amid the Scottish Highlands for all I knew. The view was beautiful— green fields, with horses and cattle grazing at will. How I envied their freedom. A farmhouse with a gravelled forecourt was nearby. Parked in front of a garage were several top-of-the-range cars. Steve's Transit was like scrap amongst the lavish vehicles.

A slender young woman with golden hair walked out onto the patio. She headed across the acres of lawn and towards an orchard. I wondered if she was Bessie and if she lived in the sumptuous cottage; it appeared warm and cosy. Grey smoke wafted from a chimney. Clean clothes on a washing line swayed in the breeze. The young girl swung a basket in her hand. I was curious to meet her, maybe she could help get me out of there? First, work—I needed fuel in my stomach.

Ben handed me a five-pronged pitchfork, a sweeping brush, and a bucket. 'Grab a wheelbarrow. C-c-come on,' he stammered.

I entered the stables, and a horrid stench lingered in my nostrils. I didn't know one end of a horse from the other.

Ben clipped a rope to a horse's harness and steered the animal towards me.

'Meet Bessie,' he said.

'This is Bessie? A goddamn horse?' I snapped. The horse grunted and shuffled its hooves, spooked by my sudden outburst.

'I-I thought you would like her. She's gentle and likes to be s-s-stroked.'

I sighed an exaggerated breath. 'Who lives in the house then?'

'Steve. His wife, Maria. Lavonia and Olivia…b-b-but you want to stay away from there. D-d-don't talk to Olivia, she'll get in trouble.' He gazed at the horse. 'They aren't gentle like Bessie. Nope, nope, nope, nope.'

If I'd had the energy, I would have slapped him. My hopes were shattered. I was curious, though, why Olivia would get in trouble and not the other girl, Lavonia.

I carried on with the daily tasks. Shovelling shit was harder than I thought. My clothes reeked of the stuff, and the palms of my hands already bore calluses. My stomach growled with greater ferocity as the day wore on. I was actually glad to see Steve arrive; he carried two tin-foiled lunches and had a large bottle of water wedged under his arm. I pleaded with my eyes for food — like a puppy, happy to see its owner return. I relished each bite; a tuna sandwich had never tasted better. I unscrewed the lid of the water bottle eagerly and gulped it down.

'Come on,' said Steve. He nodded towards the farmhouse and instructed me to follow.

Ben got to his feet.

'Not you, arsewipe,' Steve snapped. 'Eat, then get back to work.'

'B-b-but…'

'Don't fucking "but me".' Steve clipped Ben's ear with the palm of his hand. 'Now fuck off.'

As I approached the cottage, I noticed a plump woman, about forty, with olive skin and hair as black as ebony. She guided the young woman with golden hair into the back of Steve's Transit. 'Olivia's all set to go, love.' It was obvious, Olivia wasn't a relation; they didn't have their features, hair colour, or skin tone in common. She also walked with her head down, as though she felt afraid in their presence.

'I'll see you soon.' Steve planted his lips to the woman's cheek. Undoubtedly she had to be Maria, Steve's wife, but who the hell was Olivia? And where was Steve taking her…was she a captive like me?

Steve turned to me. 'Whatever Maria wants, she gets. Fuck up, and you get this!' He waved his clenched knuckles in my face.

I flinched, already familiar with them. He ordered me to remove my dirty trainers. I did as I was told and shadowed Maria into the house.

The property was amazing inside. Bohemian furnishings adorned the huge space. Lavish tapestries hung on the walls, and vibrant rugs covered the polished floor. The place was immaculate—worlds away from the trailer site. I was given clear instructions: I was the personal housemaid and cleaner of Maria, a woman with an 'I don't give a shit' attitude.

Also in the house was Lavonia, Steve's daughter. She emitted a sadness in her eyes. Lavonia didn't pay any attention to my arrival or even say 'hi', even though I was only a couple of years older. She seemed uninterested. I wanted to ask about Olivia—who was she, where she was going? Instead, I focused on keeping out of trouble. I kept my thoughts and questions to myself, so I'd get more food. For now, my assignment of general housemaid and designated cook seemed better than the alternative, plus I had access to the kitchen. Maybe I could steal the odd goodie from the fridge.

Chapter Eleven

Ben

Ben had been mocked throughout his life. His disability was a permanent reminder that he would never be accepted. People gawked at him with a mixture of pity and disgust. He felt he wasn't a person at all, but a freak. A freak who no one wanted to associate with—even his parents failed to assist him with his needs. The truth was he'd become a burden. They didn't understand that all he wanted was to have friends, to be part of something, to not be lonely.

His life was never the same again after that July evening, years ago. He'd headed to the fairground alone, twenty pounds in change rattling in his pocket. He was dazzled by the bright lights, the loud music, the thrill of the rides. A guy from inside a booth shouted into a microphone, 'Scream if you wanna go faster!' Everyone screamed with excitement. Ben loved the waltzer. He spun and spun until he was dizzy. The pumping tunes, the crowds full of cheer...he'd never laughed so much or felt as alive.

For three consecutive nights he watched the crowds and the pretty lights whilst drinking in the smell of candy floss and burgers in the air. His heart sank when he realised he'd run out of money. His mother had told him "she wasn't a money tree"; she was speaking literally, which he didn't understand, though he did know what the scowl on her face meant. A clear 'no'.

He went from booth to booth, asking the staff if there were any jobs available. He didn't want money, he wanted free rides in exchange for working. Most of the guys mocked him...one guy shouted, 'F-f-fuck off, weirdo!', mimicking his stammer. Steve had found him and put a friendly arm around his shoulder. He walked Ben away from the busy fairground and into the shadows, towards a Transit van.

'Where are we going?' Ben had asked, innocently trusting the stranger.

'You want work, don't you?'

'Yes,' said Ben, eagerly.

'Well, I've just the position for someone like you.' Steve threw his head back with laughter.

Ben laughed, too, though he wasn't sure what was so funny. As the Transit drove away, nerves trembled through his body, but he was also happy at Steve's job offer—he was sure his mother would be pleased. Steve chatted away, talking about all the animals that needed tending…horses, mainly, a few goats and chickens. Everything seemed normal, genuine. Steve appeared to be that one guy willing to give Ben a chance. A new friend.

The vehicle sped down a dimly lit lane towards a smart farmhouse.

Ben pulled out his mobile from his trouser pocket. 'I just need to text Mum, tell her I'll be late home.'

Steve snatched the mobile from his hands. 'You won't be needing that.'

Ben was confused. 'G-give it back. I have to tell my mum. I-I-I don't wanna get into trouble.'

Ben felt nervous; goosebumps appeared and caused a shiver as though a thousand tiny spiders had crawled all over his skin. Little did he know, this was the beginning of his nightmare; he would never get his phone back, and he would never go home. It hadn't dawned on him at that point that he'd been abducted, or had any inclination that he would soon become a slave to the Gypsy King.

When they got out of the Transit, Steve threw Ben's Samsung to the ground, stamping his foot on it repeatedly, the screen shattered into hundreds of tiny pieces. Ben's terrified screams filled the air; his eyes stung with salty tears, and pain rippled through every nerve ending. Steve slapped Ben around the head a few times, and immediately he cowered in submission, much like a faithful dog.

Over time, things didn't get any easier for Ben. Often, the clans disagreed, they'd use him as a human punchbag and sparring partner for both stamina and their entertainment. He hated it when the families fell out. He despised the place, but Steve would never let him leave. He tried it once and recalled his punishment—Steve and Dave held him facedown in the dirt whilst they burned his skin with a lit cigarette. His scabs wept painfully for days.

Today was a different day entirely; already he'd faced the usual taunts from the brothers. He sighed the moment he saw Lee's car parked in the driveway. Before knocking on the front door, Lee walked towards the barn. Ben knew what was coming, it had happened several times previous. Lee grew closer; Ben's heartbeat quickened. Lee was to marry Lavonia in the coming weeks, and Ben worried how he would treat her. Lee's temper was quick, and his hunched shoulders swung aggressively with every step.

'Are you ready for a kicking?' Lee spat through the gaps in his teeth.

He often assaulted Ben for no apparent reason, putting up his bare knuckles, and Ben flinched. Whether he thought it a sport, whether he was inherently evil, or whether it was just the gypsy way, only Lee knew.

Lee threw a final punch, and Ben collapsed onto the dusty ground. Lee laughed and kicked dirt in his victim's face then retreated to the cottage. This had become the norm. Every day Ben had encountered pain, cruelty, and hunger.

Once alone, Ben hit himself on the side of the head with frustration. He tried his best to get on with his work, seeing to the animals, cleaning, shovelling, and digging numerous holes. Lately, he'd dug lots of holes. They were deep—very deep—and about five foot wide. He wasn't sure what it was that Steve buried, the items were always wrapped in plastic. He didn't dare ask for fear of being struck, or worse, starved—he felt hunger often enough. He just told himself it was treasure he was burying.

Chapter Twelve

Brenton Camp

Brenton Common, located east of Doncaster, South Yorkshire, was a large grassland with areas of scrub. Although it was a conservation area of historic and architectural importance, beyond the line of sight, deep within the crevice of the hills, a hidden community took advantage of the seclusion. To some of them, this was their permanent home; to others, it was simply a resting point whilst catching up with family and acquaintances.

Within the crevice, amongst the greenery, was a gravel pathway that led to many caravans, occupied by more than fifty people. Settlers and visitors made a diverse community, with more than a hundred different gypsy and traveller families collectively forming part of the wider Romani population. They didn't think like the average Joe Bloggs, and their cultural beliefs and attitude set them apart from everyday folk even further. They followed the travellers' lifestyle and were part of a community that never asked questions and which created its own rules. Rule one was simple—to make money, by any means necessary.

Those they abducted weren't seen as human. They were only there to fulfil the community's purely selfish aims—to line the perpetrators' pockets. Truth be told, the hostages were slaves. Most of them had been abducted from the streets, some were refugees from abroad, yet all of them had a common denominator—they were forced to work their fingers to the bone, with little food and minimal comfort. They had no choice but to fulfil the gypsy clans' every whim at Camp Hell.

The nearest town was thirteen miles away, and there were no neighbours for at least twelve miles. Camp Hell was a place of fear and horror for some, a home and sanctuary to others. On foot, it was hard to locate or access; by car, security checks were carried out—but who in their right mind would enter without good reason anyway? On paper, it was registered: Brenton Common Residential Traveller Site. Appointed to assist the camp with its needs was Darren George, a liaison officer and representative of the local council.

Officially, Willow Farm was a working farm with livestock…in reality, it housed a different kind of animal. Security was tight, huge wooden gates lay at the entrance of the property, and a tall barbed-wire fence ran along its boundary. Steve and Dave were brothers by blood; between them, they had eleven children. Together, they ran their money-making schemes, ever since their dearly departed father, Shaun, left his legacy behind. Since they were young, they'd had a hand in various forms of criminal activity and the slavery trade. As adults, therefore, crime came easy to them. Loyalty to their families and the community was what made them worthy. They were motivated by greed and status. The duo and their associates made sure their operations ran smoothly—cruelty and manhandling were part and parcel of their schemes.

Travelling nomads from all over the UK turned a blind eye to the slaves' misfortune. An operation this big needed a lot of hands. Travellers from Ireland, Scotland, Wales, and further afield had similar setups in place, all funded from the same pot. Keeping such a task under wraps was much easier when you had the money, resources, and various locations to pass goods around. Some did what they did for money, others for power…many from fear of reprisals. The man on the street would call the brothers crooks, but to the travelling community, they were just living their lives the way they'd been shown.

Both Steve and Dave had a ruthless streak. They had each other's back and, they made an unrelenting duo. A team of youths worked below them, residing at many different camps; their duties would make the average person's stomach twist inside out. As long as the gypsy gang made a mint and the pounds kept rolling in, no one gave a damn.

They didn't care *how* they got their money; wealth was their sole priority. The gang had dodged the justice system for years by hiding in the shadows.

When they were questioned, corruption and manipulation saw any lines of enquiry drop. Operating without being noticed, amid a community that was, by its very nature, hard to monitor—and having several lookouts in crucial locations—meant they slipped under the radar. They'd also worked out that everyone had a price, no matter which walk of life they came from. Darren George came cheap. If they let him have his way with a few of the female slaves and paid him an annual bonus, he would keep his mouth shut. Other communities feared them. The rest of the population were simply unaware of them.

Their field of business was not for the faint-hearted. Their reward was bundles of dirty cash. Neither Steve nor Dave greatly exerted themselves, unless brutality was called for...after all, why get your own hands dirty when you have pigs to do your bidding? They say that money is there for the taking, and taking is exactly what they did, without conscience. With money lining their pockets, they were unstoppable, and willing to set up anything a punter required.

Business didn't always run smoothly, however. Darren may be a creep with his nose firmly up Steve's arse, but he had a role to play. Whenever they had a brush with the law, Darren forged official paperwork before happily accepting his bribe. Theirs was an organised crime syndicate that had plenty of muscle behind it. Over the years, their wallets grew thicker and thicker, and their sick, twisted minds became even more depraved.

Chapter Thirteen

Violence

After completing numerous household duties, Maria escorted me back to the barn. She shackled me again, like some wild beast, putting the heavy chain around my ankle. She'd already given me a stern warning, that 'any funny business and I would get it'; she'd then pulled a Taser from her pocket and waved it before my eyes. I was equally as scared of her as I was of her husband. I wondered what had caused them to be so cruel.

I sat in the dust once again; the nip in the air chilled my bones. I conceded that being housemaid to Steve's wife was a much easier job than parading half-naked in front of customers at the Gentlemen's Club or mucking out the various stables. I wondered what job I would be assigned next. And I wondered where Ben had got to. I hadn't seen him all day, and his shackle was wide open. For some time, I watched the eight-legged freaks and other insects fly and scuttle about during their daily fight for survival. In some ways, I could relate to a fly trapped in a web, inevitability on the horizon.

After a while, raised voices caught my attention. I could tell by their tone that something was wrong. I guessed that Ben was in trouble. I brought my hands up to my face and peeped through my clenched fingers. The voices drew closer, and the barn door opened. Ben received a back-hander to the side of his head, and he plummeted with a thud to the ground. His hands instinctively went to cradle his throbbing cheek. His screams echoed within the confines of the wooden structure; the brutality continued. He remained motionless, in total submission, whilst pleading for the assault to stop. His sobs fell on deaf ears. A stranger in his twenties straddled him, his huge frame pinning Ben to the ground. The guy's fists flew in an uncontrollable rage against Ben's ribs. Ben's moans were deafening and brought tears to my eyes. At one point, Ben's shirt rose, and his back bore ugly scars that looked like cigarette burns. I couldn't tell if they were recent wounds.

Where was Steve, and who the hell was this guy? I felt helpless, and my tears wouldn't stop. I couldn't intervene even if I'd wanted to; I was bound by metal chains. If I'd yelled in protest I'd have probably received the same punishment anyway. Instead, I closed my eyes and put my fingers in my ears—I didn't want to see or hear any more. How could anyone in their right mind inflict such cruelty on another? How could someone be so ugly inside and out? I was afraid of being beaten, too; my body quaked. I'd been victim to both Steve and Dave's rages before, and I didn't want a beating from this bad-tempered stranger either. It wasn't my fight or my business.

That night I lay on the cold floor, helpless and full of shame. The stranger with few teeth and a shaved head had left; his fists were still clenched, he'd walked away.

Lavonia threw her hands up in the air, seemingly disapproving of what she'd just witnessed. She'd stomped her feet and marched towards the farmhouse, yelling, 'You're such a prick!'

The guy had picked up pace in a bid to catch her up. They'd disappeared around the corner; they'd argued, though I couldn't make out what they said.

On all fours, Ben crawled along the dusty ground towards me. He picked up the chain in his trembling fingers and closed the shackle around his own ankle before placing his head in my lap. I presumed he wanted to be close for solace and warmth. His cuts and abrasions were already swelling and making their permanent mark on his pale skin. I didn't have any words of comfort. I just pulled him into my arms and cradled him like a small child, stroking wisps of his hair away from his face. In that instant, I realised there was no getting out, not ever. This torturous life of enslavement was the hand that had been dealt to me. A wave of self-pity and deep loathing for every gypsy bastard consumed me.

Once Ben's sobs had subsided and his breathing was under control, I said, 'Who was that guy?'

'L-L-Lee. He's Lavonia's boyfriend. They're getting m-married soon.'

'Lavonia didn't seem very happy with him. He's nothing but a violent thug.'

'Yeah, h-h-he's always fighting, ya know? Bare-knuckle fighting. He always wants to practise with me. I tell him n-no, but he don't listen.'

'And where's Olivia gone? Steve took her somewhere in the Transit.'

'It's Wednesday, so sh-she'll be going to see her mum.'

'Who's her mum?'

Ben shrugged.

Chapter Fourteen

Jenny and Olivia

Jenny wished time would speed up. She paced the floor of her trailer, constantly checking the window and the clock. She smoked one cigarette after another as she waited. The last day of the month was what she lived for, but Steve had mentioned something earlier that had played havoc with her mind. Plying Jenny with cigarettes, her so-called payment for her services, he'd casually mentioned that Olivia would soon be working at the club. Jenny hoped he was just tormenting her, showing his dominance, but his comment had unnerved her. Everything she did was to protect Olivia. Her daughter was all she thought about. She was the reason Jenny complied and never protested. She was why Jenny had never attempted to kill herself; she did what she had to do to survive—not for her sake, but for her daughter's.

The sound of a vehicle pulling up on the gravel road got her attention. Jenny jumped to her feet and ran to the door. 'Olivia, sweetheart, I've missed you.' She threw her arms round her daughter's shoulders. The pair enjoyed their embrace, and Jenny inhaled the familiar scent of Olivia's hair. 'Come, sit.' She couldn't bear to look at Steve a second longer, his cruel words still unsettling her. Jenny didn't want it to be true and she strived to ignore the smug grin on his face. She stood tall and struggled not to show her irritation, as he loved watching her squirm.

Steve didn't speak. He closed the door, slid the bolt across, and walked away. Even though the women were subjugated, it brought Jenny some relief when he bolted the door. It wasn't so much that he locked them in, he shut the rest of the world out.

'How have they been treating you at Willow Farm?' she asked Olivia.

'Just the same.' Olivia paused. 'Well, Lavonia's okay. She doesn't treat me bad, but she doesn't speak to me, either. You know what Steve's like…he has a temper like a boiling kettle on a hot stove. And Maria, well, I'm just her general dogsbody. She's a hard-faced, foul-mouthed bitch.'

Jenny's emotions quickly turned to concern. 'You'll have to do better at Willow Farm. Go that extra mile, make it so that

Maria can't cope a second without you. It's a big place, after all.'

'But why, Mum? What's wrong? I do what I'm asked and I don't complain.'

'I don't really want this to be true, and I didn't want to mention it either, but…' A sinking feeling took hold. '…Steve mentioned something about working you at the club. I'm not sure if he said it just to ruffle my feathers, but I need to prepare you, just in case.'

'No, I can't. I won't! You said I'd never have to do that. I just want to get out of here.' Tears welled in Olivia's eyes.

'Don't you think I want to get out, too? Get us both far, far away from this hellhole? It's difficult.' Jenny cuddled Olivia to her bosom, her arm cradled around her baby's back.

'Difficult is living this way. We have no freedom of choice. We're slaves. I'd rather die than become a whore…and, for God's sake, stop babying me!' Olivia pulled away from her mother's embrace and turned her back on her.

She couldn't believe what she was hearing, but then again, what did she expect? There were no hearts and flowers at Camp Hell, only orders, restrictions, and misery.

Chapter Fifteen

Duties

Early the next morning, Ben and I were feeding the chickens when Steve's Transit came speeding up the narrow lane. Olivia got out. She didn't scream or run in fear, and she appeared to have a normal conversation with Steve. She walked alone back to the farmhouse without supervision. I envied her freedom and wondered who her mother was. She didn't have the distinctive gypsy look, but I was still curious to know if she was also a prisoner, held captive against her will. If so, who was her mother, and why did she get special treatment?

It became clear that I'd only been covering household duties in Olivia's absence. I was a little jealous that she got to work and stay in a warm house that was bug-and-dust free, eating homemade food. Olivia went inside, and Steve reversed the Transit until it was in front of one of the outbuildings. He opened the van's back doors before undoing the padlock that secured the building. As he opened it up, fluorescent lights glowed. Dave stood guard beside Steve with what appeared to be a gun in his hand. My mouth dropped—it was the first time I'd seen a weapon so close.

Five young men of Chinese origin, all thin and gaunt, appeared from the outbuilding. Each carried hessian sacks over their shoulders. Dave pushed the barrel of the gun into one guy's back, prompting him to walk forward; the others followed in sync, loading their product from the unit to the van. I tried to not make it obvious I was watching them. From the corner of my eye, I tried to figure out what was inside the sacks.

Dave said, 'The harvest better be well and ready for cultivation.'

It was clearly not corn; it had to be drugs, most probably cannabis. The five guys were then marched into another outbuilding. This one was dark; I guessed they were hanging up the harvested bud to dry, ready for the curing process. Once finished, the door to the outbuilding was locked behind them. I wondered if the young men had been ripped from their families by traffickers and forced to work. Judging by the fear they displayed when Dave waved his gun about, there was no way it was a voluntary working relationship.

It was hard not to think about them. I considered if they could speak any English and who was feeding them. They appeared seriously malnourished, but I had my own cross to bear on that front. I carried on with my duties, cleaning up the animal filth in the barns. It wasn't my business to ask questions, I was too afraid. It didn't stop thoughts swirling around my mind, though. What the hell was going on? Prostitutes, drugs, and now guns…this wasn't a typical gypsy racketeering scheme, this was undoubtedly hardcore, organised crime. I feared I would die there, by the hands of one monster or another…maybe by an overzealous punter or even through starvation. I had to get out, but how?

Chapter Sixteen

Clues

Even though it was just after 9 p.m. and out of working hours, Crane ventured down the corridor in a bid to find out any information regarding 'Jackie' or 'Jenny', or whatever her name was. What was her association with the gypsies? It could prove a dead end, but in his field, any information was worth checking out. He knocked on several doors; some residents didn't even bother to answer, which was to be expected—not because of the time of night, but because of the ignorant ways of that particular area towards law enforcement. Luckily for Crane, the inhabitant of Flat 209 had much to say.

Linda invited the detective in. Crane sat on the couch, which was surrounded by porcelain dolls. He wondered what made a woman of a certain age collect such hideous things. Dolls gave him the creeps, with their wide eyes that followed you around the room, no matter where you stood. He pulled his eyes away from the monstrosities and cut straight to the chase.

Linda was forthcoming; he quickly learned that the mysterious woman's name was indeed Jenny. Jenny Ward, who had lived in the block with her daughter, Olivia. Linda seemed relieved to speak to him and couldn't stress enough that she was happy someone was finally investigating Jenny's strange disappearance.

She sat with a vodka on ice in the armchair, sipping it after every breath as she voiced her concerns. 'I reported that Jenny had disappeared to the police years ago, but no one seemed to take my claims seriously. The police checked the premises and said that a few personal items had been packed. There were no signs of robbery, hence the rumours of a moonlight flit.' Linda stared at her glass. 'I always blamed myself, you see. She wasn't just my neighbour, Jenny was my friend. After I met Big Kev on the internet, I sort of encouraged her to get back into the dating game.'

'Was she dating someone when she went missing?' asked Crane.

'All I know is she met some guy named Steve on Plenty of Fish. They went out for a date, she came home to the sitter, then she and Olivia were never seen again.'

'Who is this Steve?'

'I don't know. A woman in the hair salon said she'd seen Jenny in a club on the last night she was seen. She was with a guy called Steve. He's apparently a traveller.'

'Do you think Jenny ran off with the gypsies?'

'Not likely,' Linda said firmly. 'She was just getting her life together. She wouldn't have disappeared without saying goodbye.'

'Have you got a picture of Jenny. Or her daughter?'

Linda scrolled through her phone. 'We'd get together about once a month, have a bottle of wine, a little chitchat, while the kids played. She's probably changed a bit since then.' She paused. 'Here's one. I can print it out for you.'

'That will be helpful,' said Crane. 'Thank you.'

Within moments, Linda had printed off an A4 portrait of Jenny with her daughter on her knee. She handed the picture to Crane. 'So, you believe the rumours, that she fled with her kid in the middle of the night, are bullshit?'

Crane was tactful. 'It's a possibility, but it's too early to say.'

'She had no reason to run. She'd just started a university course. It just doesn't make sense…' Linda trailed off.

Crane took this as his cue to leave and allowed Linda to walk him to the door.

Chapter Seventeen

The Red Velvet Curtain

The next day I was taken to the Gentleman's Club. I peered through a crack in the office door, trying to eavesdrop on Steve and Jenny's conversation. It wasn't much of an office. On the desk was a CCTV monitor showing the entrance to the club.

Jenny was clearly upset—her arms were doing all the talking, and her voice got louder. Steve didn't approve of her outburst. He grabbed her by the hair and dragged her off the stool to her feet. The discussion turned from heated to sour within moments. It was then that I realised Jenny was not one of them, she was just another pawn in their sick, twisted games.

His hand still firmly entwined in her dark locks, Steve swung his free hand and slapped Jenny across the face. She didn't scream or call out for help. Instead, she glared at him with utter disgust.

'I told you last week, she's coming of age. She's got to pay for her keep, somehow,' he spat through gritted teeth.

'You promised Olivia wouldn't be used in that way. That was the deal from the start. I've spoken to her, told her to work harder at Willow Farm. She doesn't want to come and work at the club, I don't *want* her working at the club.'

'I don't care what you want. I don't give a flying fuck. You work for me, you do as you're told. You keep moaning that once a month isn't enough…if Olivia was here permanently, you could mould her into being a whore, just like her mother!'

'I don't want her to be a prostitute. She's my fucking daughter, you bastard!'

'Call me what the hell you like…bastard, dick, cunt.' He laughed at Jenny's discomfort. 'She's coming on Friday. I don't make deals with whores, I make money off them, so you better get her trained.'

'You can't break your word. I've done everything you've ever asked of me…sold myself and coached innocents into hookers to protect her. You promised you wouldn't harm a hair on her head.' Jenny sobbed and pleaded with Steve to change his mind.

'I don't think you're in a position to bargain,' he sneered.

'Please, please! Not Olivia. I'll do anything,' she begged.

It was clear from Steve's brutality and his twisted smirk that he had no intention of giving in to Jenny's request, whatever their previous deal. He was not about to set her or Olivia free. It was horrific to listen to, then I realised that I needed to be more concerned about my own safety. I was back in the godforsaken club to be coached into being a sexual object. That's when the light in my mind switched on...if Olivia was Jenny's daughter, could I use this information as a bargaining tool to stay in her good books? Maybe I could put together an escape plan for us all.

A tap on my shoulder, and I jumped out of my skin.

'Go and get ready.' Dave pointed towards the red curtain.

I silently complied and walked away slow and stiff, zombie-like, fearing what lay behind the velvet fabric. Pulling it back was like revealing another dimension, a hidden world of sin.

I was kitted out in heels and a flimsy outfit once again. My eyes must surely have displayed fear, and my body felt numb. Reality was more chilling than the cold temperature. The other girls scuttled about in unison, a formation of worker ants; they didn't engage in chitchat. Their heavy makeup didn't fully conceal their bruises. It was obvious that Steve, Dave, and the punters had no remorse; it was even sadder to think that the paying customers probably had families...daughters of their own. What kind of sick pervert paid a backstreet club for sex with teenage girls? The customers shared a commonality — they barely acknowledged that the girls were human.

Jenny was on the prowl, clipboard in hand, directing each girl into side rooms. Her eyes were red, her earlier upset visible. Her hands trembled. I wanted to speak to her, to tell her that all of us had to escape, but I wasn't sure I had the guts, or whether it was the right moment to address what I'd overheard. I followed her footsteps, waiting to be assigned to a room. More pressing things were on my mind.

When I found the courage to peer into one of the many rooms, I couldn't believe what I saw. My jaw all but hit the floor. An Oriental girl, about eighteen years old but possibly younger, was on her knees. She was being yanked by her long ponytail across the carpeted floor by an overweight, faceless man in a weird, black rubber suit. Her naked body squirmed at his rough touch; her limbs were a tangled mess. She screamed and yelped and dragged her feet in protest. Her tiny frame was no match for such a monster.

Laughter escaped from behind the guy's mask. In one swift action, he lifted her to her feet then tied her wrists and ankles to the wooden posts on the bed. I couldn't stand to look a moment longer. I felt sick, faint...my legs weak as though they would give way at any moment. I didn't want to be part of this. I clenched my shaking fingers into a tight ball. Maybe I could use my knuckles... The reality was, fighting back wasn't an option. I had to get out.

We continued down the hallway. Everything I'd dreaded beyond the red curtain was worse than I'd imagined. Even my darkest fears had not prepared my mind or my eyes. It was as if time had frozen as every horrific detail came slowly into view.

Several rooms lined the corridor, each numbered from one to ten. The smell of stale alcohol and sweat filled the air. I masked Jenny's footsteps as though I was her shadow, my eyes and ears on full alert. As we passed room three, someone moaned. I didn't want to admit to myself what was really happening behind the door, and what was likely to happen to me. Stepping forward, I caught the echo of torturous screams. I trembled, terrified at what the young female was enduring at the hand of some sick customer. A punter came out of a different doorway, leaving the door slightly ajar; a young girl was bound to the bed, her arms and legs spread wide and her head lolling listlessly from pain and exhaustion. Blood dripped from the corner of her pink lips, her dark eyes appeared lifeless, and there were signs she'd received painful lashes across her stomach. It was obvious she had been brutally punished.

'I can't do this,' I spat, not through fear but anger. 'Why can't you help me? Help the girls, Jenny, what the hell is wrong with you?'

'I can't,' she said, then raised a finger to her lips, warning me to be silent.

'Don't you mean you won't? You allow these girls to be tortured…for what? To save Olivia? How's that working out for you?'

Jenny swung her arm through the air, and her palm slapped against my face. 'You know nothing, stupid girl.'

'I know about Olivia,' I said defiantly. 'And you know what? You're just as bad as them.'

Chapter Eighteen

Side Room

I quivered with anxiety, and vomit threatened to escape my throat at the thought of the beastly guy in the room, putting his old, wrinkled hands on my young skin. Jenny closed the door; I thought I saw a glimmer of sadness in her eyes.

The punter appeared to be about sixty. His hair was thinning, and his skin had mottled-brown ageing spots. 'I want a blow job,' he said, matter-of-factly, dropping his pants to his ankles.

It could have been worse, I told myself. It wasn't penetration, or any weird, kinky stuff the other girls had endured. I dropped to my knees, in front of him, my stomach churned. He smelled like old furniture, and a whiff of talcum powder clung to my nostrils; it was as though I could already taste him. His shrivelled skin was growing.

'Do it,' he insisted and thrust forward his hips.

I had to swallow back bile. I didn't want to take his manhood in my hand, let alone my mouth. I closed my eyes and visualised being somewhere far away, somewhere over the rainbow, where blue birds and witches fly. Yet all I could think was, *I'm melting…my body and soul, diminishing.*

'I can't, I'm sorry,' I cried and stared up at him with pleading eyes, hoping he would see me as a human, or maybe someone young enough to be his granddaughter. I hoped that his conscience would be stronger than his sexual will.

'I've paid good fucking money for this, whore.' He grabbed my hair at the roots with both his hands and yanked me forward.

The moment his skin touched my lips…it happened so fast. I bit down hard. He screamed. I released his cock from between my teeth. His blood dribbled off my chin.

Only his screams registered. He swung his arm and landed a blow that knocked me sideways. My ears were ringing from his punch as well as his bellowing. From behind me, a hand was placed over my mouth and an impossibly strong arm grabbed my waist. I hadn't even heard the door open, but I didn't have time to turn round. Steve picked me up and carried me out. My mind screamed, but I remained silent. His grip squeezed my ribs; I couldn't breathe. Steve was shouting obscenity after obscenity. I'd really gone and done it this time.

Jenny came running up the corridor. 'What's going on?'

'This bitch has just taken a chunk out of a punter,' Steve snapped.

'I'll see to her, Steve. I need to talk to her, baby steps. I guess it's my fault, I haven't prepared her properly.'

'Talking's over. I'll show her what's she's got to do. She's going to learn the fucking hard way. Go and send my apologies to the customer. Give him a freebie, just make it fucking right.'

I was thrown onto a bed in another room. Steve slammed the door shut with the heel of his foot. I scuttled towards the headboard, trying to put as much distance between us as possible. My body shook; I could hardly breathe, let alone make a sound. I was petrified in mind and body. Steve removed his jeans and pants and threw them aggressively on the floor. He forced me to lie flat, launching his weight on top of me and ripping my panties off. The sting of him between my legs was painful and inconsiderate; he penetrated me. He showed no emotion, and my body moved involuntarily with his every thrust. It hurt, an agony like nothing I'd ever experienced before…sharp, stinging, a pure unrelenting suffering. The violation lasted for what felt like forever although, in reality, it had been only minutes. He laughed when he climbed off me whilst I sobbed, my body and soul shattered. The tears wouldn't stop. I was broken, left with an unbearable aching pain in my groin. There was blood smeared across my inner thighs.

I'd been raped. I cried like I'd never cried before.

'Aw, did it hurt? Poor, poor Amber. I'll tell you what hurts, you not lining my fucking pockets, giving my business a bad fucking name. So, now you know the ropes…what the punter wants, he gets.' His words were as raw and as twisted as his actions.

I tucked up my knees and lay in the foetal position, cradling my stomach. Steve had torn me into a million pieces. I couldn't look at him; I hated him, and I hated myself. He left, and I scrubbed at my skin with my fingernails, I wanted to rid the dirty, unclean feeling that lingered, but it was no use. I crumpled into a pit of anguish and depression.

Sometime later, I froze, holding my breath. Someone entered the room. Maybe if I pretended to be asleep, whoever it was may leave me and let me rest. I'd rather be dead than have some random guy treat me like a piece of meat. It wasn't a guy, it was Jenny. She perched her bottom on the bed and leant her head against my shoulder, offering some form of comfort.

'I'm so sorry, Amber,' she whispered in my ear. She stroked the side of my face, wiping away my tears.

'If you're sorry, you'd get me out of here. You'd get all the girls out of here.'

'It's not that easy.' She sighed.

'Why not? You have more freedom to roam than the rest of us. I've seen a phone in the office, you could call the police.' I sobbed.

'You don't understand. They'll hurt Olivia.'

'I understand perfectly. As long as Olivia is okay, they can rape, beat, and starve the rest of us.'

'It's not like that…' said Jenny. She went quiet, as though the truth had just hit her.

I hauled myself up by the elbows and looked her straight in the eye. 'Tell me then, what's it like? You are so full of shit. Wait till they have Olivia laid on her back...let's see how you cope with that.'

My words seemed to strike a chord and pull at the one shrivelled black heartstring Jenny had left. 'You're right,' she replied, her face full of anguish. 'Olivia is coming here on Friday. Steve said she has to, and...' She didn't finish her sentence.

Her eyes welled with tears and, for the first time, I actually saw the real Jenny—a woman afraid, concerned, broken and destroyed.

'Jenny, we have to get out. All of us.'

Chapter Nineteen

Links

A combination of cocaine and exhaustion wasn't a good mix. Crane didn't sleep well that evening or the evening before, waking in cold sweats after nightmares. When would his pain ease? He was at the stage where he beat himself up, rambling in a state of confusion, amid a mass of dark, haunting memories he couldn't shake. He needed a boost, something to numb the pain. He took out a credit card from his wallet and a small, clear plastic bag containing white powder. He rolled up a twenty-pound note and followed the white lines, sniffing hard at the substance until his nostrils throbbed from the tiny clumps.

He lay back on the settee whilst the buzz kicked in. For a few moments his heart raced as the stimulant corrupted his bloodstream. Half an hour later, he was dressed in his grey suit, with an energetic, artificial confidence, ready to step out the front door.

He walked into the station, holding his head high. His fellow officers scuttled out of his way. Fucking morons, the lot of them. He sat and placed his Costa coffee on his desk, then searched the database. It wasn't possible for a mother and daughter to vanish into thin air without any questions asked, but that's what had happened to Jenny Ward—she'd simply disappeared off the radar. He looked deeper; her daughter hadn't been registered with any schools in the area, either.

Maybe her finances could hold the clue. Her benefits had been paid into her bank account every fourth week and been collected for some time from a post office on Albion Street—at least, until the benefit renewal date where no fresh claim was made. Her disappearance just didn't add up. Where was Jenny Ward and her daughter? And who was Steve? It was no use checking with the post office; the account had been closed years ago. Maybe the council's gypsy liaison officer had heard of a Steve. Could Jenny and Steve be connected to the missing foster home kid, Amber? Crane's head swirled like a boiling mass of spaghetti. He could be wrong about the whole thing, but a dog with a bone wouldn't give up; something told him to keep digging in that direction.

He scrolled through the council's directory on his laptop. Darren George was named as liaison officer for the gypsy campsite on Brenton Common. It could be a lead. Crane scribbled down the guy's number on a piece of scrap paper and punched it into his mobile

It rang for a long period, then a voice said, 'Hello. Sorry I'm away from my desk. If you care to leave a brief message and your name and contact number, I'll get back to you as soon as possible.'

Crane waited for the beep and left his rank, name, and number.

Chapter Twenty

Wake-up Call

Jenny felt as if she had the weight of the world on her shoulders. She couldn't help herself or her daughter — never mind the rest of the girls. She looked at the phone in the office; Amber couldn't have known it was out of service. If only it was that easy, simply phoning for help. She couldn't see a light at the end of the tunnel. She tortured herself by counting the hours, minutes, and seconds until her daughter, Olivia, was set to join her in this godforsaken place.

Amber's words had been a wake-up call, and they'd rattled around her head all day long... 'You have more freedom to roam, you can get us out of here.' Amber was wrong, Jenny was a hostage herself. Yes, she did have more freedom in some ways, but over the years the violence and brutality she'd suffered had shaped her. She didn't have a choice, she just concentrated on surviving another day. Yet she couldn't help thinking that the change of circumstances simplified her dilemma. Could being reunited with her daughter aid their escape? The more Jenny thought about it, the more she saw possibilities, though she acknowledged that it would be terrifying and difficult. As reason and doubt battled in her head, a failed escape would result in severe, painful punishment, or even death. But what could be worse than this? Her heart couldn't withstand the pain, she couldn't—she wouldn't—stand by whilst these beasts offered her child up to perverted strangers.

As a dark cloud of anguish continued to hover above her, she resigned herself to the fact that Olivia would never go back to Willow Farm. That shortly, she would have to watch her own flesh and blood lie on her back and become a whore, a slave to every dirty bastard out there. As her mother, she would have to find an inner strength to save them both, at the first given opportunity. Maybe she was just fantasising. Maybe it was her way of coping with the situation, but in that moment, she convinced herself that working and residing together could actually be the key to getting the hell out of there. Maybe she could save her daughter and the other girls, if not herself.

Chapter Twenty-One

Digging for Unwanted Truths

B en didn't like what he saw; he could tell the situation wasn't good. He felt uneasy—all he could think about was his mother and father, homemade food, his comfy bed. He wasn't bothered about the fairground rides anymore, he just wanted to go home. But he wasn't home, and he wasn't safe.

Years later, his situation hadn't changed. He was still captive, still at the mercy of the brothers and their moods. The Transit drove to the outer perimeter of Willow Farm, metres away from the boundary line. Ben had hidden treasure there for Steve and Dave before. It was vigorous labour, digging a large hole by hand, but Steve told him to work hard and dig faster, then maybe he would get a burger. His salivary glands were already flooding.

Ben pushed his foot with force onto the head of the shovel, only stopping to mop the sweat from his brow. The brothers helped him retrieve the parcel wrapped in plastic packaging from the back of the Transit; it was big and heavy, much like the others. They heaved, swung, and dropped the parcel into the hole. It landed with a thud, dust rising. Once the dirt settled, something…something long and pale, protruded through a rip in the plastic wrapping.

Ben's eyes widened, and his jaw dropped. He couldn't help staring at the pallid flesh of an arm—the arm of a dead body. Even though he was mentally slow, it quickly hit him like a shockwave to the brain…it wasn't treasure he'd been burying, but human corpses. He let the shovel fall but couldn't stop the unwanted surge of liquid coming up his throat. He vomited. His hands trembled, and he cried, his thoughts frantic. Who was this person? Were they male or female? He assumed male after seeing the biceps in the arm, the large hands and stubby fingernails.

'Pull yourself together,' warned Steve, 'or you may end up being buried next to him.' He laughed.

Ben didn't want a kicking, or worse, to be buried there, too…with the bugs and the worms, where no one could bring flowers like he'd done for his grandma as a child. He didn't dare ask questions—he was scared of the answers. He picked the shovel back up. With every flick of dirt, his mind worked overtime, exploring every dark thought imaginable. He was afraid, more afraid than he'd ever been; this was more than a beating, this was murder. Still, he covered up the evidence, shovel by shovel, whilst his heart grew heavy. His instincts told him this was wrong. He patted down the last bit of earth, his emotions exploding. He hyperventilated. His upset manifested into rage. He gripped the wooden handle on the shovel tightly, and his knuckles turned white. He wanted to swing at Steve and hit him hard over the head. Whoever this dead person was, they didn't deserve to be murdered and dumped in an unmarked grave.

Ben raised the shovel, ready to swing, to knock Steve's head off his shoulders, but Steve noticed his intent.

'Just fucking try it, boy,' he growled.

Instantly, Ben was brought back to reality. What was the point? The perimeter of the grounds had huge iron gates and high barbed-wire fencing. Dave was also sitting in the Transit van. He wouldn't get away with it. Ben tossed the shovel to the ground with one thought…would death in an unmarked grave be the only way he'd escape this hell?

'I can't d-d-do this anymore. It's not right.'

Steve had clearly had enough of Ben's defiance. Even though Ben had thought better of attacking him and dropped the shovel, Steve was not going to tolerate his outburst. Steve closed the gap between them and grabbed Ben by the throat, squeezing hard, his cheeks turning purple.

'Can't do it or won't do it?'

Ben felt the spit from Steve's words on his face.

Steve's temper appeared to rise like a red mist. He could snap Ben's measly neck in one action, but the sound of hooves and a voice from behind seemed to bring him back to the here and now.

'Dad! What the hell are you doing? You're going to kill him!' screeched Lavonia, sitting bareback on her favourite horse, Bessie.

Steve wouldn't want Lavonia to learn about the body in the shallow grave. 'Go back to the house,' he ordered, his tone firm, though he released his clenched knuckles from around Ben's neck.

Ben's knees buckled as he gasped for air; he went dizzy, faint. In that moment, he realised something. He didn't want to die, he wanted to live. He wanted to go home.

Chapter Twenty-Two

Wedding Jitters

I t was the day before her wedding. Lavonia had only gone to find her father to finalise some last-minute details, or maybe, subconsciously, she'd wanted to tell her dad that she didn't want to marry Lee after all. Surely the Gypsy King would put his own daughter first? Her thoughts were obvious to her, it wasn't possible, her father's cruelty had confirmed it. There would be no get-out clause for her.

Lavonia couldn't stop thinking about what she'd witnessed, her father treating Ben with such unkindness. He had a ruthless streak that could corrode silver. Then there was Lee, the bad-tempered bare-knuckle fighter, who used any excuse for a punch-up. Her emotions were all over the place, and her heart sank to the depths of no return.

She thought about other brides she'd seen on TV and her cousin's wedding. How the bride was full of excitement, whereas Lavonia only felt dread. She wasn't excited; it was duty, her family honour at stake, nothing to do with what she wanted. She wasn't in love, either.

Marrying her cousin wasn't on her list of priorities, but it had already been settled amongst the families and arranged, after a hellish year of courtship. They were often chaperoned by prying eyes, not that Lavonia cared, she didn't want to be alone with Lee. He wasn't pleasant in looks or personality, and the thought of kissing him, with those missing teeth, turned her stomach. To be truthful, Lee was a total arse, always acting the big man—he reminded her too much of her father. Lee had won her father's heart, a chip off the same block, two peas in a pod, and he'd apparently already saved enough money to buy a trailer for them to live in on Brenton Common, which had sealed the deal.

Lavonia recalled the day the elders met and gave wedding counsel, after Lee asked her father for her hand in marriage. The elders' strong, binding words had stuck with her: 'Once you are married, you can never leave each other.' It was a devastating blow, although Lavonia could not disobey her father's wishes, even if she'd wanted to. With Lee's family now on the campsite, the relations came together. The families celebrated around an open fire with music and lots of stewed meats and ale. The thing with the gypsy way was, no

Romani code was written down anywhere; it was only kept alive by actions and tradition. Time never seemed to move on or modernise. Lavonia thought the traditions were outdated. She'd wanted to pick her own husband, not be part of a gypsy clan deal. The old ways were not what she'd dreamt of.

Lavonia had to face facts, that, once the ceremony started and the elders wrote her name in the large book of records, her life was over. She'd become a clone, following in her mother's miserable footsteps. She wished tomorrow would never come. For now, she plastered on a fake smile and pretended to enjoy the night's festivities.

That day, Lavonia had travelled back to Brenton Camp. Her relatives and family's friends had arrived from far and wide, their trailers all parked up closely on the campsite. The men gathered around an open fire and drank beer greedily, toasting Lee and his success at 'getting his leg over with a fine catch'. That evening, she'd sat in her grandmother's trailer and listened to the travellers' wives giving marital advice.

'Tend to your man, fill his belly and give him plenty of children!'

Lavonia had nodded, though her mind was elsewhere. She wanted to get out, make her own decisions, but how? She thought about all the places she wanted to visit, the friendships she wanted to make, and how much she'd enjoy being self-sufficient. Why wasn't she allowed to get a job and a little flat somewhere with a garden, and explore her opportunities on her own terms?

The more she listened to the general chatter, the more the jitters took over. She needed some space to clear her head. She jumped to her feet and headed towards the door; she was sure all the colour had left her face and she felt a sickness accumulate in her stomach.

'What's wrong?' called Maria.

'Nothing, Mum, I just need air. Think I've a bit of a headache,' she lied.

The caravan erupted into laughter, and someone shouted, 'You'll need that headache excuse once you're wed.'

The campsite was lively and cheery, but it didn't reflect how Lavonia felt on the inside, defeated and sad. She walked through the camp under the moonlit sky with thoughts of running away. Everywhere she turned, some family member sang her and Lee's name. Her world was quickly closing in on her...she wanted to hide, but the campsite was overrun; she wouldn't get a moment's peace.

As she approached the shadows, she noticed the trailer which the young girl, Amber, had been thrown into, the girl who had spent a few days working on the farm. Lavonia wondered if the trailer was empty; it would be the perfect place to get some alone time. Peering over her shoulder, she slid the bolt across. Everything was dark, and it smelled of damp. She turned on her phone's torch and looked around. On the floor lay Amber, huddled in a ball, without a blanket or pillow. She appeared cold, thin, and exhausted.

Chapter Twenty-Three

Lavonia

I tried to adjust my eyes to the darkness that surrounded me, a blanket of deep, dark despair. I couldn't stop shaking, and my breathing became rapid. Would Steve not let me rest? My body was exhausted, and my mind was fragile. I strained to make out the silhouette peering at me from the doorway.

'Leave me alone!' I yelled.

It wasn't John—I hadn't seen him for a few days. It wasn't the right build for stocky Steve or lanky Dave, either. The small figure was unfamiliar.

I put my hand up to my eyes, shielding them from the bright artificial light. My heart raced, and I felt much like a wild animal, that had been cornered, and about to be in the grasp of yet another predator.

Except this wasn't a predator at all, more a bird with clipped wings. Someone similarly fragile and broken.

The door closed. 'Hello.' It was a female. Her tone appeared to be friendly, though her voice quivered.

Should I answer her? Instantly, my anxiety rose—was this some sort of trick? A mind game? What did she want? I lay on the cold floor, weak and helpless, trying to find the strength to speak. 'Aren't you Lavonia?'

'Yes.'

I sat up and straightened my clothes, trying to appear more like a young lady than a cheap hooker. I considered what she wanted—this wasn't the usual routine. Had she brought food and a drink? My lips were sore from dehydration, and my ribs had begun to protrude through my pale skin.

'Is there a light in here?' she asked, waving the torch on her phone. Her voice had a distinct Irish twang.

'No.'

'Oh, that's good. I don't want to be found.'

I wasn't sure if she was a friend or foe, but she was on her own and her wicked father was not in sight. Her mobile could actually be a lifeline. I cut to the chase and asked, 'What do you want?'

'To hide.' Lavonia sighed heavily as she sat at the table. She turned off her torch, and we were once again in total blackness.

'Why are you hiding?' I probed. 'From what? From whom?'

'It's a long story. I didn't know where else to go.'

I got to my feet and sat opposite Lavonia, even though I couldn't really see her. It was nice to have company. 'Well, it's not like I'm going anywhere.' In any other scenario, two girls of a similar age would have enjoyed chatting about the world and their worries, but under the circumstances, it wasn't a pleasure. I couldn't look past the fact I was a prisoner and that Lavonia was the Gypsy King's daughter.

'I don't really want to talk about it,' she said quietly.

'It can't be that bad, whatever it is.'

'It's family. You know how it is, having to…' Lavonia didn't finish, but I could tell she wasn't happy.

'I don't really know that much about family. My mother replaced me with her one true love, heroin.'

'Oh, gosh, I'm sorry. Is that how you came to work for my father? You didn't have anywhere to go?'

'Not quite,' I said. Surely she wasn't that naïve? Maybe she was just in denial.

'Why are you locked up in here? What work do you do for my father?' she asked matter-of-factly.

I couldn't tell if this was a ploy by Steve to cause further hurt or if Lavonia was genuine.

'Different things.'

'I've seen you a few times on the farm with Ben. I feel sorry for him, but what else can I do?'

'Is Ben okay?'

'He was when I last saw him. My dad gives him a hard time. It's such a shame…he's disabled, you know. He works long hours without complaint.'

'Yeah, I know that. So, you don't know what your father does for a living? For real?'

'It's not a gypsy woman's place to know a gypsy man's business,' Lavonia said drily. She sighed again, clearly burdened with her own troubles.

As we chatted, it became clear that Lavonia was oblivious to most of the goings-on at Camp Hell. She had no idea I was a slave or that I'd been kidnapped from the streets. I shared my sorry story, and she shared hers, telling me of her arranged marriage to her cousin, Lee. My mind whirred with possibilities—maybe we could help each other. But if I planned any kind of escape, I'd have to get the others out, too.

I had no alternative, I had to ask, 'Do you think you could help me escape?'

Lavonia hesitated. 'How am I supposed to do that? We have a site full of guests. You know my family will disown me if it all goes wrong.'

This would be my only chance. I had to, somehow, get her onside. 'What if you run away with me? You don't have to get married then. You could call the police, you have a phone.'

'Do you know what they will do to me if I involve the police? The last gypsy woman to go against the code was set on fire in her own trailer.'

'That's disgusting,' I said, shocked but not surprised. 'It's inhumane, Lavonia. It's murder.' When she didn't respond, I said, 'Give me the phone then,' and I lurched forward to take it from her.

'I'm sorry, Amber, I just can't.'

I could tell she felt bad about the situation, but still she stood and left me alone. The bolt slid across the door, and again I was alone in the dark, only dreaming of escape.

Chapter Twenty-Four

The Gypsy Code

It was a Friday, and security was sparse at Willow Farm, with all the gypsy clans at Brenton Common for the wedding. Ben had been left all alone, shackled in the barn, until the celebrations ended.

He thought of the last time he'd been chained up, when the family was away having a good time. They'd left him for two whole weeks with minimal resources, whilst they sunned themselves abroad. Eventually, they'd arrived back, with big bellies and bronzed skin; he hoped it wasn't going to happen again. Then, he'd thought he was going to die from cold, hunger, and dehydration. His energy levels depleted, and his body became a bag of bones. He'd hardly had the strength to sit, never mind stand, and the manacle had created unsightly blisters where it had been secured too tightly.

He hoped the wedding would be over quickly and that Steve would bring nourishment for his empty stomach. Ben thought about his old life, the one where he received regular meals and hugs from his mother. He thought about the police, and he often wondered if they knew he was missing. Did his family miss him as much as he missed them? He recalled the last time the police had shown up at Willow Farm. Steve had been furious, though Darren had managed to tip him off that the cops were on their way. He'd also told Steve that the person who had leaked information was an elderly gypsy woman called Rose Marie.

Rose Marie had become ashamed about what she'd witnessed. The gypsy clans weren't sticking to their natural roots or heritage; in her mind, they'd become fuelled by cruelty, status, and money. The day after the police raid, Rose Marie's home was set alight; she was still in it. Her screams rang out all over the camp. No one dared intervene, they just stood and watched the orange flames grow without batting an eyelid. Steve had warned the other travellers that they would receive the same treatment if they, like Rose Marie, failed to stick to the gypsy code.

'Grassing to the police goes against the crust,' he'd said.

Ben knew that the gypsies' way of life was not for the faint-hearted, and also that no one ever got out alive.

Chapter Twenty-Five

Lies

Staring at his mobile as it rang, the caller's number withheld, Crane debated whether he should answer it. He didn't quite feel himself; he needed another fix. Being in the office, amongst prying eyes and with a busy workload, he'd not had a chance to calm the storm that threatened to take over his twitching body. He sighed heavily, thinking of how and when he could snort his poison. His stash was running low, he needed to obtain more—to do that, he had to work to pay for his addiction.

With money on his mind, he slid his finger over the screen and accepted the call.

'Hello, Detective Crane? It's, erm, Darren George here, liaison officer at Brenton. I believe you want to speak with me. How may I help?'

As an experienced copper, Crane sensed the unease in Darren's voice. He gave him the benefit of the doubt—maybe Darren was nervous about speaking to a detective.

'Why don't you tell me what you're investigating?' Darren mumbled. In his head, he chastised himself. *Pull yourself together, Darren! Relax. Find out what this copper wants, try to inform the others.* Darren knew how crucial it was that he didn't say a wrong word. Beads of sweat formed on his brow. It was imperative that he gave just enough information to ease Crane's mind. The last thing he wanted was the Old Bill sniffing round the place.

There was an awkward pause. Crane didn't want to give Darren any unnecessary or sensitive information. 'It may be something or nothing,' he said, 'but do any of the travellers at Brenton go by the name 'Steve'?'

A lump formed in Darren's throat. Genuinely, there were a few Steves at the camp, though he knew damn well which one the detective was enquiring about. Whatever Crane was looking for, Darren needed to throw him off the trail, away from the dealings of the Gypsy King. There was too much at stake—namely, his back-handers. He also feared repercussions; he was being paid a hefty sum to protect the site and its people within his remit.

'Yes, we have a few Steves. It's a common name. What's the issue, I'll see if I can help?'

'Is there a Steve who's connected to a Jenny Ward? She has a daughter, too.'

Darren went silent for a moment, thinking about what to say next. The colour drained from his face, and he was glad they were having this conversation over the phone. Of course he knew Jenny and her daughter. This wasn't good. He had to think fast. 'No, Jenny Ward doesn't ring any bells,' he lied.

'What about Amber Hart?' asked Crane.

'Erm, nope…that name doesn't sound familiar, either,' Darren said in a hurry before hesitating again. With a crack in his voice, he added, 'I'm familiar with most of the travellers who reside on Brenton, but so many come and go, it's sometimes hard to keep track. I can ask around and, if the names do arise, I'll certainly come back to you.'

'I'd appreciate that,' said Crane. His years on the force told him that Darren was hiding something. The tone of his voice, the way he'd garbled his words then hesitated. Crane didn't want to spook Darren; their whole conversation had not satisfied his curiosity—if anything, it had raised his suspicions. If he wanted to know what was going on at the Brenton site, he'd have to visit himself.

As soon as their call ended, Crane jumped in the car and called a familiar number. Thirty minutes later, he was parked up near an alleyway, where goods were passed to him through a gap in the window, in exchange for the £150 Crane paid. He watched as his source raced away on a pushbike, a hood masking his face.

Crane hid the bag of white powder in his glove compartment after separating what he needed to get him through the next couple of hours. Tapping the powder onto his clenched knuckle, he inhaled deeply, until the taste stung the back of his throat. Just a few moments later, his head felt straight, and adrenaline willed him on. He started the engine, turned up the radio and, with his foot pressed hard to the accelerator, he headed towards Brenton Common.

Chapter Twenty-Six

Olivia's Arrival

Jenny had been given clear instructions "not to fuck up" in Steve's absence. With the wedding preparations going on, she'd been left to run things for a few days. The bouncers were Steve's eyes and ears; they were legitimate, they hadn't been abducted or held against their will. They were just as bad as the organisers, though, strutting around in their black suits, flexing their steroid-enhanced muscles, turning a blind eye to the hostages' misery. Jenny had learned fast that money and sex constituted the root of all evil. The bouncers were paid tax-free, cash in hand, with the bonus of a girl of choice after an evening's work. It never failed to disgust her that a free blow job and dirty cash was all it took to silence some men.

She paced the floor. The club was due to open in an hour's time, and she was anxious. Olivia would be arriving shortly, and Jenny's stomach was in knots. Every time the door opened she looked over, her heart beating so hard, it may jump through her ribcage. She wanted to get out of this hellhole as fast as her legs would carry her, but without Olivia it was no use. Her mind spun full circle… *We are never going home, never breaking free. We have to get out…but how? And when?*

Her thoughts were interrupted by a commotion. She glanced over her shoulder discreetly, not wanting the other girls to notice the chaos that must be written all over her face. Dave stood before two female slaves who sat together in a corner of the bar. With the lights dimmed and from the other side of the bar, it was hard to recognise which girls they were, but Dave snatched one of them by the hair and dragged her to her feet. Jenny recognised the screams instantly. Olivia! Goddamn, how did she get in undetected? How long had she been there?

Jenny sprinted from one end of the room to the other, watching Dave coil his knuckles into the roots of her daughter's hair until her scalp could take no more. The sound of her daughter screaming was a stab, like an arrow had penetrated through Jenny's heart. Olivia reached out to her mother and called for help, her athletic body buckling under

Dave's rough touch, her long, golden hair tangled in his fingers, her baby-blue eyes full of fear.

Jenny momentarily froze, as though everything in the room had come to a standstill, her daughter's distress ricocheting in her ears. Olivia's deafening screams turned to uncontrollable sobs; she pleaded for Dave to let go. A surge of adrenaline rattled through Jenny's core; she seized hold of Dave's hand, clawing at his fingers so he'd release her daughter from his grip.

'Let go of her!' she screamed.

Dave wasn't the type to take orders from a slut. How dare she lay her hand on his? With his free hand, he hit Jenny in the mouth with force. A surge of blood burst from her top lip.

'Please, no. Please…' Jenny begged, '…it's her first day.' She ignored the fact that her own face needed stitches. 'She just needs to be shown the ropes.'

It was clear, from his brutality and twisted smirk, that Dave relished in their distress. It wasn't the gentle reunion Jenny had imagined; she'd hoped to keep Olivia out of harm's way for as long as possible, hidden out of sight. The whole ordeal was horrific, and she was crushed mentally and psychically.

Time stilled, minutes rather than seconds. Dave finally released Olivia from his grasp.

'I was just showing her the ropes myself, toughening her up. She's going to have to get used to a bit of rough and tumble, she's not a housemaid anymore. Go get her dressed into something more revealing…the punters love a newbie.'

Dave's grin stretched from ear to ear. A vision of her sticking a knife into his gut flashed into Jenny's mind. She cupped her arm around her daughter's waist and led her away, gesturing to the other girl to follow.

Once they were in the back room, Jenny held Olivia close. 'I'm so sorry,' she whispered and snivelled.

'I can't do this, Mum,' said Olivia, sobbing uncontrollably.

Chapter Twenty-Seven

Freedom for John

John writhed in pain. He knew there was no way out. He'd lost a lot of blood; it seeped from an open wound on his head. It dripped through his fingers and onto the ground around him. He became light-headed; his strength left his body, and he drifted into unconsciousness.

Sometime later, he woke in sudden shock, trembling from the temperature outdoors. He was frozen to the bone. He was alarmed to find he'd been stripped naked whilst comatose. He shivered and wondered why this was. What the hell was going on? Grey smoke drifted with the brisk wind. What the heck was Steve and Dave burning, and where were his clothes? John was worried, it hadn't been a normal day; work had been extra challenging and had not gone as planned. He struggled to get to his feet; the day's heavy grafting had done further damage to his already broken back. He couldn't shovel tarmac or carry a brick.

As he slowly climbed into the back of the Transit, every nerve in his lower back screamed in pure agony. Dave hadn't been impressed, not that he expected either brother to show any consideration or sympathy. In fact, Dave put his foot down on the accelerator so they hit every road bump, which brought John further pain.

The van charged through the open roads towards the campsite, its speed matching Dave's temper. He ranted, 'You were on a daily rate, and you couldn't even last a few hours. You fucking worthless piece of shit.'

'I'm sorry,' said John, grimacing. 'My back's gone.'

Once inside the perimeter fence of Camp Hell, Dave didn't stop the van at the usual drop-off place. He pulled onto a grassy embankment, turned off the engine, and dragged John from the vehicle.

'What's the point in flogging a dead horse?' he snarled.

As soon as his wicked tongue spoke, a baseball bat he'd taken from the van connected with John's skull. He instantly passed out.

When John came round, he couldn't get up. His back had spasmed, and his legs felt as though thousands of tiny pins and needles were stabbing him. He surmised that he was suffering from either a trapped nerve or a prolapsed disc. Neither was good.

It suddenly dawned on him that the brothers were burning his clothes. A thought stuck in his mind, something repeated many times by the other slaves—once you were unable to work, you were disposable. The brothers would leave no evidence that you ever existed. A word caught in his throat; he was unable to say it, but it screamed to him within…MURDER.

John lay helplessly whilst the brothers came towards him. He closed his eyes and said a silent prayer as blood trickled from his skull and ran down his face. He knew what was coming. His heart raced, but his body surrendered. A click of a trigger, and the impact was sharp, penetrating. A single bullet aimed at his heart exploded through his chest. John's eyes sprang open. Instinctively, he brought his hands to the wound, and warm blood oozed through his fingertips.

It wasn't the departure he'd hoped for, but he accepted that he was finally free. He looked at the blue sky. A flock of birds soared. In a way, he was soaring, too. Death was better than the life he'd suffered for years at these bastards' hands. Death was his escape, and he didn't fear it anymore. He'd been liberated from his pain.

John's body still warm, his clothes nothing but ash, the pair tossed his corpse into the back of the van before driving to Willow Farm.

Chapter Twenty-Eight

Clients

Overcome with anxiety, I tried to ease my disturbed mind while I readied myself for the next client. All I could think about was Steve and his brutality when he'd stripped me of my innocence. The room was sparse, as were my clothes. There was a single chair, a small table with an assortment of sex toys, a window with iron bars, and a bed covered only with a heavily stained base sheet. I wasn't sure if I should sit or stand; irritated, I sat on the chair, and swung my legs, my nerves threatening to get the better of me.

Shortly after, the door is thrust open. I could hear Jenny, but I couldn't see her. I wondered if her shame meant she couldn't face me. She guided the punter through the doorway. Once the door shut again, my heart raced. The punter was already taking off his trousers, followed by his pullover, then his boxers. He left his brown socks on, he knew the drill. There wasn't any chitchat; I just looked at him, my wide eyes screaming silently, but no discomfort showed in his middle-aged features. He hadn't come for a blow job or hand job, he informed me, he wanted full sex. He patted the bed beside him. I didn't want to remove my clothes and lay myself bare for him, even though the thin material of my dress did little to cover me. On the other hand, I didn't want another beating, or Steve inflicting another vicious assault on me. Slowly, I went to step out of my heels, but the client ordered me to keep them on. I crawled on all fours onto the bed then turned so I was flat on my back.

I concentrated on the Artex ceiling. The guy's fingers reached for my panties. He yanked them from my groin, guided them over my heeled feet, and dropped them to the floor. My breathing became more rapid, and I think he could tell I was ready to scream. He grabbed something from the table; it was a dirty cloth that he stuffed into my mouth to muffle any sounds. I struggled to breathe. His muscles bulged; they supported his body weight above me. His cock was hard; the sting of him felt like a hot poker between my legs. My body quivered and squirmed at his touch. Eventually, I gave in and simply lay there, broken,

I tried to fight back my tears. I followed the detail in the ceiling, in a bid to think about anything other than what was

140

happening. I focused on the white-washed walls, stained from years of filth, the lightbulb covered in cobwebs. The smell of sweat was strong. The client's rhythm became faster until, eventually, he was spent.

He collapsed on top of my tiny frame. The cloth was still in my mouth, and my lungs literally gasped for air. He climbed off me calmly without giving me a second glance. He put on his clothes and shoes then left.

I pulled the gag from my mouth and immediately threw up what was left in my stomach. I staggered to where my clothes were, in a state of shock. I felt dirty, violated.

This was Hell. I had to get out of there…soon.

Chapter Twenty-Nine

Another Punter

After that, it was one stranger after another. I feared there was no getting out of Camp Hell. I didn't want this life, I didn't want to be a piece of meat to some paying punter, but what choice did I have? The flimsy green velvet dress I'd been given was short, and it clung to my scrawny frame as I wobbled about on six-inch heels.

The punter eyed me from head to toe; he smiled, seemingly happy with what he saw. He patted the mattress, instructing me to sit. I just wanted to get it over with quickly. God only knew what Steve would do if I refused. The previous guy had been bad enough, but this one stank of cheap cologne, although it wasn't powerful enough to mask the stench of bacon and fried food on his skin. He obviously owned or worked in a café...probably a greasy spoon, looking at his cheap trainers and the egg stain on his shirt.

He caressed my legs with one hand. His skin was rough against my silky, smooth legs. He stroked my greasy hair, and suddenly, I was consumed with anger towards every living thing. His body was relaxed, mine was tense. He grabbed the hem of my dress and peeled it from my skin. He ran his grubby fingers over my pert breasts before squeezing hard at a nipple.

I wanted to scream, 'Get the fuck off!', but fear pinned me to the bed.

He moved his hand to the bud between my legs and forcefully entered me. I gritted my teeth and squirmed a little, tears streaming down my face. I tried again to find a spot of interest on the ceiling. Time seemed to still. The punter pumped back and forth repeatedly. Pain ricocheted through my every limb. It hurt, it was torture...sore, rough, inconsiderate. He soon stilled, his body weight crushing my petite frame. The sting of him burned like molten rock from a volcano. In that moment I crumpled into bleak desolation; it was the darkest place I'd been. I lay, feeling like I'd been ripped apart at the seams. My blood turned cold—this was the third time I'd been violated. First, Steve, the second dirty bastard, and now this randy old dog. The peak of my nightmare—they say bad things come in threes.

The punter got to his feet. He didn't speak, only grunted. He picked up his clothes and left me lying there, broken. Memories of his putrid aroma and his touch would forever be embedded in me. I turned to face the wall, pulled my knees up to my stomach. The images wouldn't leave. I sobbed and sobbed. I knew, deep in my heart, that this was only the beginning, that I would be brutalised on a daily basis. I wasn't cut out for this. Who would be? How did the other girls manage to perform every day? Did they have nerves of kryptonite and a body made of steel?

Chapter Thirty

Bad Thoughts

I woke the next morning back in the caravan, still feeling like I'd been ripped at the seams. My body ached; I was alone, scared and hurting. I'd started to believe that humans were hideous, they were evil; I'd learned this firsthand. I would never forget their cruelty, their taste, their scent, it was almost as though they'd taken parts of me, piece by piece. They'd entered my body and broken me. I thought about death...would it be immoral to wish to die? I'd been touched by many, against my will. I never wanted to see another person again. Conversely, I longed for human company. I hadn't seen John for days. Even though he'd been a man of few words, I missed him. Apart from Ben, he seemed to be the only man who didn't want to take something from me. We had a connection—we were both slaves, and our sorrow was parallel.

He'd previously said that this shell of a trailer had been his home for years, so where was he? I was concerned about his absence; was he ill? Had Steve stationed him in another location? I hated to think about it, but maybe he was dead. I thought about the last time I'd seen him. His weight had diminished, his pale skin appeared almost grey in colour, and the exhaustion on his face was clear. Yet he never complained. I should have really asked him about his previous life, how he'd come to be there. Then again, did I really want to know the finer details? His time as a slave at Camp Hell had been lengthy. Just thinking about that had me doubting that I'd ever break free. Perhaps it would be easier for me if I just accepted my fate and grasped that I was trapped. That I was indeed a prostitute, and Steve was King Pimp.

Consumed with worry, I rubbed my stomach, which sparked even more dark thoughts. No way, I couldn't be...I didn't want that. I retched at the thought of falling pregnant to any one of those perverts. There was no way I wanted a constant reminder nor the burden of a baby; I couldn't look after myself in this place of torment and sin. I hadn't been offered birth control and wondered what became of pregnant girls and their babies in this hellhole—surely it must have happened? The thought unnerved me; maybe Steve had connections to backstreet abortion clinics. Maybe impregnated mothers had their young torn from their arms. Maybe the babies were simply dumped on someone's doorstep, maybe Steve flushed the evidence down the toilet or sold newborns on the black market. Maybe pregnant mothers were murdered in cold blood.

Those thoughts knocked me sideways. I was petrified; it was a situation over which I had no control. My mind felt more and more tainted with every wicked thought, a place like this did that to you. I sobbed until my eyes ran dry. I hated waiting for the unknown to happen, hated being shipped around, raped, tortured, and starved. I felt as if I'd fallen into a dark abyss. If only I could climb out of this bottomless pit of deprivation.

Chapter Thirty-One

Following a Hunch

They say that money is the root of all evil, but, to Crane, the truth was a lot simpler: it was man and his selfish desire. The gypsy clans were hard to keep tabs on at the best of times, with money lining their pockets, their lips sealed, hidden secrets, and a site that was hard for any regular person to penetrate. Crane just needed his suspicions confirming. A stirring in his gut told him something was amiss.

A forty-minute drive later, and Crane pulled up at a huge set of iron gates. Behind them lay a community of gypsies that didn't accept regular folk meddling in their business. The gypsies had a code to uphold—they wouldn't speak ill of each other. Crane had to see things with his own eyes, snoop around, ask a few questions. He needed to know if his suspicions were correct, if Darren was indeed covering for a certain Steve—and why?

It was his legal right, as a member of the police force, to be granted access, though he also considered that his presence wouldn't be welcome. A metal padlock blocked access with his vehicle, but it wasn't going to stop Crane sniffing around. He accepted full well that not all gypsies were thieves or rogues; most of them held wholesome family values and had a good work ethic. Why on God's earth would Darren not be forthcoming when it came to simple facts? Why had his voice quivered; what was he hiding?

Crane opened the glove box and stuck his index finger into a bag. He rubbed the coke on his gums and put the bag away securely before exiting the car. He could have done with a pair of trainers to climb the fence, but his brogues would have to do. He hitched his leg over the top bar and jumped to his feet on the other side, his knees stinging a little as he landed. Being over forty had its downfalls.

He walked along a dusty, makeshift road. There were tethered horses on both sides, and a horde of trailers stood in the distance.

Chapter Thirty-Two

Planning

It was well after midnight when the girls gathered in the dressing room to change from their slutty outfits into their day clothes. Jenny peered over her shoulder to make sure no one was listening as she spoke to them. It wouldn't end well if the bouncers heard.

I watched Jenny with the girls. Her mask had slipped. Jenny wasn't cruel, she was just doing the best she could under the circumstances. Maybe her daughter's return had pricked her conscience; maybe she'd been beaten so often and pushed so low that she'd forgotten she had one. Her eyes gleamed with determination. The others listened to her encouraging words. I felt some hope, as though a weight was slowly being lifted. Jenny informed the girls that escaping wasn't easy, that the risk was high, that it could even be deadly. The girls were in total agreement. It was worth a try; anything was better than being hookers and slaves to these gypsy bastards.

The monsters had already stolen our virginity, our freedom, and our lives. We'd already lost everything and encountered suffering on a daily basis. None of us wanted to die, but we didn't want to live like this, either. Dying would at least be a release if this was all our lives would ever be.

Although Olivia hadn't yet been brutalised, it was going to happen sooner or later. Jenny had no option—if she wanted to save her daughter, she had to act fast, no matter what the cost. Jenny knew full well she couldn't keep Olivia hidden in the storeroom forever, it was only possible because Steve and Dave weren't around. The bouncers were clueless, and Jenny strutted around as though it was any other evening. Olivia's peachy skin, golden hair, and athletic body would definitely cause a stir and attract unwanted attention. Her good looks would be a curse in this godforsaken place.

The girls didn't complain that evening whilst paying clients abused their bodies. They didn't struggle to recall the first time their fragile bodies had been used and abused; the memories were burned into their minds, bodies, and souls, and could never be forgotten.

I put my arm around Jenny. 'I really admire your courage,' I told her. 'We can do this as a team.' I couldn't help thinking of Ben and the Chinese guys who were undoubtedly still locked up at Willow Farm. I worried about John, as it had been a while since I'd last clapped eyes on him. Hopefully, we could save everyone.

So, it was decided…whilst the wedding took place, Jenny would cause a stir to distract from, and aid, our escape. The night wore on, it was all I could think about, the thought of the wind whipping around my face, running across open land and breathing in the God-given air. Freedom was on the horizon, like the sun shining in all its glory. I'd danced naked that evening for a group of groping punters of every ethnicity. I'd been forced to suffer their grubby fingers skimming across my skin; even though their eyes and hands had ogled and groped me, I was thankful it wasn't their cocks I'd had to endure. That evening, wobbling on those heels, it had been easier. Easier to block out the abuse and the hurt, now that I had something to focus on: escaping.

That same evening, the bar closed, and I didn't linger like I did usually, hunting for leftover nuts and crisps. I changed quickly into my day clothes and walked at a fast pace, knowing that freedom could be less than twenty-four hours away. I turned the corner…would this really be my final evening at the club? Not that I wasn't glad to see the back of it.

I headed towards the staircase, waiting in line silently with the rest of the girls. We were escorted by the bouncers into the back of the Transit. I gazed at the moon in the distance, and its light gave me a glimmer of hope. We clambered in, the usual routine, except it was the first time since I'd been abducted that I felt any emotional warmth. Us girls huddled together, an uneasiness in the air.

Chapter Thirty-Three

A Cold Welcome

Crane was agitated. He should have snorted a few lines before walking this far—already, fatigue washed over him. He fumbled to smooth his hair in the breeze, his mind clouded by thoughts. He knew the task before him required more patience than force. He wanted to meet Darren face to face, get him onside. Turning up, unannounced, would ruffle his feathers, but Crane's instincts told him Darren was hiding something.

The campsite was jam-packed with trailers and more people than Crane had imagined. It was like a whole different world. Children roamed free, as did dogs of mixed variety. It was clear some sort of celebration was taking place; travellers from far and wide had come to participate in the event.

It could be the fairground coming to town, Crane figured, or they were gathering for the horse fair. Something beautiful and unique caught his eye—an old gypsy wagon made from walnut and pine, known to the community as a vintage vardo wagon. It looked to be from another time, with its intricately detailed outer shell. It was highly decorated with beautifully engraved carvings and paintings and ornate wheels. The gypsy women were dressing it with flowers and ribbons...maybe a wedding would be taking place shortly, he surmised.

As he took in the vardo's beauty, all eyes were on him. The air seemed to turn sour, and for a brief moment, he questioned whether returning to the force had been a good idea. He couldn't withstand another beating. His state of mind was too fragile, his pain ran too deep.

Yet he also knew that, if he solved the case, he'd gain back some respect from his colleagues at the station. Such a result could be the answer to his suffering. It was almost as though confronting a site full of gypsies, lawless and law-abiding, was a test of his strength and abilities. Maybe he was wrong about the whole thing...drastic circumstances often required drastic actions. The visit wasn't entirely 'on record'; sometimes, investigations...well, you had to follow your gut.

As he ventured further into the camp, it quickly turned from bustling to a total standstill.

A young voice shouted, 'Hey, fella, what do you want?'

The kid had a runny nose and no shirt on his back. His stance was confrontational, his hands on his hips, as if mimicking an elder peer.

'I'm looking for Steve,' said Crane. He thought he may as well throw the name in, see what would come back.

'Steve who? And who wants to know?' came another voice.

It was strange. All of a sudden, the playing children and their mothers disappeared into their homes. Doors where shut and blinds dropped. Crane was quickly surrounded by an angry mob.

'You can't just show up here. Who the fuck are you?' said a lanky guy with a shaved head and muscle top.

Crane had to think on his feet. He realised his presence wouldn't be appreciated, but he couldn't understand why he was receiving such a hostile welcome. Beads of sweat accumulated on his forehead; he was twitching for another fix. He pulled out his ID and waved it in the air. 'I'm Detective Crane. I spoke with the liaison officer and was hoping to catch him. Is he about?'

'He's not here,' said the lanky guy. 'If you've spoken to him, you'd have surely made an appointment at his office.'

'Well, now I'm here, do you mind if I take a look around?' Crane prompted.

'Have you got a warrant?' The lanky guy smirked and crossed his arms.

'No.'

'Well, fuck off. We're in the middle of wedding preparations.'

159

Crane had to face facts; he wouldn't be able to gain access without going through the proper channels, so he turned on his heel. The mob seemed to follow him; they made sure he kept to the mud path and didn't stray. As he got in his car, a Volvo sped down the lane. Its tyres stirred up the dust; it was obviously in a hurry. The Volvo pulled up, and the guy who jumped out extended a hand.

'Darren George. Nice to meet you. I just got a call to say there was some kind of disturbance. You know how it is, even the police can't go about harassing or discriminating. What's the problem?'

'The problem is, you know who 'Steve' is,' said Crane.

Darren's cheeks turned scarlet. 'Look, there's one Steve here, the Gypsy King. I feel you have some kind of prejudice.'

'And I feel you're a liar,' snapped Crane. 'Why not say that in the first place? So, is Jenny, Olivia, or Amber Hart here?'

'Come and sit in the cabin. Let's see if we can clear things up, and I'll see what I can find out.' Darren felt pressured. The cops usually informed him of any raids or concerns. They didn't just show up. This guy was ballsey. He had to speak to Steve as soon as possible, see what plan of action needed to be taken. Crane's visit wasn't authorised, and Darren suspected that the detective was just chancing his arm.

Chapter Thirty-Four

Hostage

Crane sat in the cabin, waiting for Darren to come back. If Jenny had run away to join the gypsies, why didn't the liaison officer just say so? He'd also lied about knowing Steve. Crane needed to find hard evidence. The hairs on his neck told him all was not well, but the thought of leaving with no clues irritated him. His mind flicked to the bag of coke in his glove box, but he couldn't let his hunch slip through his fingers. He was eager to prove himself to the rest of the force and make overdue arrests; maybe his drug-addled mind was leading him on a wild goose chase. In all his time on the force, he had learned to take notice of what his instincts told him—he was onto something.

Footsteps approached, and raised voices drew closer. He crossed his legs in a bid to appear relaxed, though sweat ran down his spine. He didn't want a fight, just a lead in the right direction. When the cabin door sprang open, a vile taste accumulated in the back of his throat. He gulped. Darren wasn't there; instead, two powerhouses of sheer muscle stood menacingly. One was stocky, and the other guy was the lanky one he'd previously spoken with. It was clear from their scowls that this wasn't a social call. He was in trouble, big trouble.

Crane jumped to his feet. He put his hands up and calmly said, 'Look, I don't want any trouble. I'm here on official business.'

'Fucking bullshit,' spat the stocky guy. 'No one knows you're here.'

A lump filled Crane's throat. It was true, not one of his colleagues knew of his whereabouts. He'd never been one for logging his location. It was clear the gypsies knew this and that they had an inside man. He had underestimated the situation, that much was obvious. If he could have kicked himself, he would have.

Everything happened so fast. Like they were in an old western, the stocky guy moved his stance from one leg to the other and pulled a gun from his back pocket. He pointed it at Crane's forehead. 'Move,' he ordered.

Crane experienced the same fear he had felt all those years ago, when he was brutally assaulted by the gang of young thugs. The gun at his head prompted him to follow instruction, and he shuffled his feet.

He was ushered between the pair and forced into the back of a Transit van.

'Empty your pockets,' the lanky one growled.

Crane turned them inside out, reluctantly handing over his car keys and phone. What choice did he have? He'd been a fool. He quickly scanned the area, looking for an escape route. He couldn't see one. Maybe he could run or pick up something heavy to fight the duo off. He had to face facts: he couldn't outrun a bullet. As he stepped into the back of the van, Darren appeared in the distance. He stood with his hands on his hips, seemingly unconcerned that the two meatheads were kidnapping a copper.

Crane had been able to tell Darren was a lowlife from the very start, but he'd never expected to stumble onto something so big. It was obvious the goings-on at the site were not lawful, and that these particular gypsies were higher in the criminal world than he'd anticipated. Clearly, Darren was a snitch and on the payroll of the gypsy gang.

The engine started, and Crane was forced to steady himself with his hands on the inside of the vehicle as the van bounced along the rural roads. The air inside smelt of tobacco, booze, and sex. The stereo blasted rock music, blocking out the voices of the two thugs in the front. Crane knew he'd made a huge error. Maybe it was inevitable; obviously his drug habit had clouded his judgment. A restlessness took over his every limb; he was unsure if it was due to the impending brutality he was likely to receive or if his body was craving another fix it wouldn't get. He couldn't tell which was worse.

Suddenly the vehicle stopped, which threw Crane off his feet. He took a deep breath…had he been driven to a private location, away from prying eyes, to take a bullet in the head?

Chapter Thirty-Five

Wedding Day

The day had come, though Lavonia wished it hadn't. She craved a different life, a life filled with choices and her own decisions. Her mother made last-minute alterations to the wedding dress; it resembled a meringue to Lavonia, a large white cloud, and it was completely over the top. All she could think was that she'd look ridiculous. The dress was as hideous as her partner who'd been chosen for her.

The trailer was crowded with aunts and cousins, everyone fussing and clucking like hens. Lavonia would have preferred to be back at Willow Farm; she would have taken Bessie for a ride to clear her head and galloped through the fields. She probably wouldn't have returned. She wondered how Bessie was doing, which triggered thoughts of Lee, her husband-to-be.

Lee had spent his stag night at Willow Farm with some of the lads—cock fighting, drinking and, most probably, bare-knuckle fighting. As if it wasn't bad enough, marrying a toothless yobbo, she was curious to know whether an evening of drinking and fighting would have added more scars and bruises to his already beaten-up features. She found his missing teeth a turn-off. He was also missing a personality, she thought. Lavonia had no choice but to keep the family happy, further securing family ties and keeping traditions alive. It sucked.

Though she didn't want to speak to Lee, she didn't want to let her father down either. It was a no-win situation, so she pulled out her mobile and clicked on the group chat. What kind of mischief had Lee had been up to? A video had been posted several hours ago. With her phone in her hand, she stepped out of the door. 'I'm just going for a walk,' she insisted.

The women around her were knee-deep in thread, flowers, and jewels.

'You can't go now! You're about to have your hair and makeup done,' said Maria.

'For God's sake, Mum, give me ten minutes to breathe!' Lavonia stomped down the steps and headed for a quiet spot beneath a tree. Clicking on the video, she couldn't believe what her eyes were witnessing.

Ben was, apparently, the entertainment at the gypsy boys' stag. It began mildly, but quickly turned cruel, and it ended with devastating results. Lee was drunk, riding on Ben's back, whilst the latter crawled on all fours, his knees and palms bloody. The boys cheered and threw lasso ropes in the air, as though they were at a rodeo. Lavonia felt sick, and her hands trembled. She wanted to turn it off, but at the same time, she wanted to see the end to make sure Ben was okay. How could they treat someone like this, he was disabled, for God's sake? One of the lads managed to hook a rope around Ben's neck, and the group's cheers moved up a level. Ben was dragged across the dirty barn floor; he was sobbing and fearing for his life. Lee took the other end of the rope and climbed several haystacks. The others followed. Once at the top, he bounced from foot to foot and held up his arms in jubilation—like Stallone's scene on the steps in *Rocky*. He then tossed the rope over a wooden beam.

Four of the boys, with Lee leading, pulled and yanked at the rope like they were playing tug of war. They hauled Ben's body up high in the air, and then suspended him, his feet dangling metres above the ground. The rope squeezed his tiny throat, and the muscles in his neck were clearly bulging. Ben was screaming, his legs kicking wildly.

'Let him go,' Lavonia yelled at the screen.

Her mind in turmoil, she watched Lee tie the end of the rope to a metal peg, which left Ben hanging in the air. His face was twisted in agony, and his eyes looked like they were ready to burst. His skin turned blue, his tongue lolled, and his head slumped to one side. The camera then focused on the guests below who were chanting, 'Kill the freak! Kill the freak!' The view suddenly altered position, to that of the floor, as though the phone had been dropped.

The video ended.

Chapter Thirty-Six

Home Truths

I was locked in the trailer again. John was nowhere to be seen. I'd been given a cheese sandwich and a bottle of water; they lasted at least three minutes. I huddled in a corner, my knees up, trying to get some rest before the 'big event'. I felt cold, scared, worried. Would the plan work, could it actually happen? Due to the wedding, we would have a change of escort to the club. The bouncers would collect us all whilst the family and their guests were at church. I guessed Steve didn't want every traveller knowing his cruel business—he probably wanted to keep his slave-racketeering-cum-pimping efforts a dirty secret. Maybe it wouldn't look good.

The escape plan wasn't set in stone; I needed to show a little faith. Jenny had been adamant that she was going to get us all out through the back door by starting a fire. I hoped the whole place would go up in flames, though I didn't want the fire-fighters to have to pull our crispy, burnt corpses from the debris. It was the only idea we had, under the circumstances. It was a risk worth taking. I went over the finer details in my head. Was it doable? Though clouded with doubt, I also felt exhilarated that we were at least trying to escape.

My thoughts were interrupted. I froze; the bolt on the caravan slid open. I anticipated John, but it was Lavonia. She was as white as a sheet, anxious, distressed, and her eyes were red.

'What's wrong?' I asked, concerned. Maybe I shouldn't have cared and only been worried about my own safety.

She struggled to speak; the words seemed wedged at the back of her throat. She was sobbing so hard, and her chest heaved frantically. I was in no position to offer her assistance. All I could do was lend her an ear. I'd listened to how devastating her life was…I'd wanted to yell, 'Try being a slave!'

She stood there, shaking, and thoughts sprang into my mind. Maybe it was selfish of me, but I couldn't help thinking, *I hope to God she goes through with the wedding and doesn't foil our plan.* We didn't need any hiccups.

'It's, it's Ben. He's…' She mumbled something, wouldn't finish her sentence.

My heart sank just thinking about him. 'He's what? Sick?'

Lavonia waved my words away. 'No! He's dead.'

'He can't be,' I said, though I don't know why I thought it an impossibility. I could tell by her wailing that it was true. 'How? When? What happened?'

'Lee hung him,' she sobbed. 'I can't marry him...he's wicked, and so's my father.'

My mouth gaped. I processed what she'd said. My stomach twisted into knots.

'I have to cancel the wedding,' she continued. 'I can't...I don't want to.'

Her whining was getting under my skin. Were her tears truly for Ben or her own circumstances? I grabbed her shoulders, trying to shake the truth into her. 'You're all sick. Cruel monsters. You can stop this.' Rage threatened to take over my entire body. All I could think of was Ben's face, his innocence...and that the bastards had murdered him. 'You have to get us out, stop this cruelty.'

'How the hell can I stop this?' she bawled.

'You have to help us get all the hostages out. You don't want to marry Lee? Then it's time to grow a pair. Do the right thing and stop wallowing in self-pity.'

'I need time to think. I didn't plan for this.'

'You think I planned for this? Being holed up in a filthy trailer and pimped out every night, just so your dad can pay for his big farmhouse, his trailers, your nice horses, and your fancy fucking wedding?!'

Lavonia turned to walk away. Her mobile stuck out of the back pocket of her skinny jeans. I stepped forward and grabbed it, it one quick swoop.

'You're one crazy fucking bitch,' I screamed at her. 'You can call the police, get us out!' I waved the mobile in front of her eyes whilst trying to slide my finger across the screen.

She leapt forward and tried to prise my fingers off the phone. We wrestled, until she bent my fingers back into an unnatural position; my grip loosened, and she took the phone back.

'You don't understand,' she pleaded, 'I can't call the police. I'll be disowned…or even killed.'

'Poor fucking you,' I spat. 'You're a coward, and if you marry Lee you're already dead.'

I could tell my words had got to her. She opened the trailer door and slid the bolt across from the outside.

I panicked. What if she told her father about my outburst? What if she cancelled the wedding? What about Ben…where was his body? Why had they done that? I fell to my knees in a heap, realising how disposable our human lives were to these bastards.

Chapter Thirty-Seven

Confrontations

Crane suffered cuts and bruises to his face and body. After the attack, he became a prisoner like everyone else, locked up in a trailer. His self-esteem plummeted. His knuckles were busted, his nose bled, and his sanity hung by a thread. The beating had been a repeat of when he'd been set upon by the gang of youths. He was weak on all levels, but, he told himself, at least he hadn't been shot.

Though beads of sweat lined his brow, his body trembled violently with the cold. His muscles spasmed with cramp, and his whole core was awash with fatigue—the effects of the coke fading.

He didn't know how long he'd survive within the confines of the tin walls. He was overcome with vivid, unpleasant dreams, and the walls closed in. Aches and pains ricocheted through every nerve ending, his mind in turmoil; he'd really gone and blown it this time. A restlessness within him couldn't be stilled, no matter where his mind took him. His body called out for a fix, a need to reach oblivion, to subdue the agonising pain, for anything that stilled his body.

The shame, his reputation as a cop on the line, and deep despair felt too familiar. Irritation raised its ugly head again; he was frustrated by his needs, frustrated by his circumstances…no way would he be mocked again, he'd rather die. What did he have to prove? His worth? His sanity? He had to accept that, this time, he was a hostage, a pawn, a deadbeat. He wasn't a hero, he was tarnished. All his life he'd been set up to fail, his peers had concluded that fact on a regular basis. What was the point in punching the walls? His knuckles had swelled and become bloody. Should he just accept his fate?

Reality came crashing down on him like hallucinogenic nightmares. He was an addict. His addiction was not the antidote—maybe this diabolical situation was the remedy to ending his need, not a whipping from a studded paddle in the hand of a paid madam. Maybe it was time for confrontation…to confront himself, the battle within. He had to tackle his fears head-on, his raw emotions, his overwhelming feelings of isolation and self-loathing; they all played a part. He had to battle the demons whether they came in the form of man or addiction. There was no rainbow, Crane had hit rock bottom. He asked himself, could he clamber out of this dire situation?

Chapter Thirty-Eight

A Blazing Situation

The bolt slid across again, and I hoped Lavonia had seen sense, that maybe she had rung the police and done the right thing. Just get me out of here, I pleaded silently, help us all.

Lavonia seemed distant. She was a wild mess, even more so than when she'd appeared earlier and told me the devastating news about Ben. Her hands trembled. There was a distinct smell in the air of some sort of fuel. 'Run!' she urged. 'Get out as fast as your legs will carry you.'

The flick of a lighter was all that was needed to ignite her petrol-soaked body. Her screams, the smell of her flesh, the terror on her face—I'd never forget them as long as I lived. Her body turned into a fiery inferno. Noise escalated across the whole campsite. Screams, chaos, and unrest filled the air. A group of people ran towards her, yelling in fear and panic. Her whole body quickly became engulfed in flames; the blaze glowed brightly, the flames blue, yellow, and orange. I froze, staring at her face as she writhed in excruciating pain. She held her arms out towards me, as though she'd done this for me, to aid my escape. I wondered whether I should intervene, take off my jacket, try to put her out, or should I just run for my life? My mouth was moving, but I wasn't aware I was screaming.

Steve galloped towards his daughter. He pushed past the crowd, knocking folk sideways, a huge bucket of water spilling with each frantic step. He threw it over her, but it wasn't enough. Her skin seemed to melt away.

'Water, water!' he yelled, distressed, before collapsing to his knees.

Watching him hurt and hysterical, I still couldn't drum up any pity. All I thought was: *You did this. Your cruelty. Your love of money clouded your judgment. Even your own flesh and blood couldn't stomach your savagery.*

They say karma is a bitch…watching Lavonia burn was hideous, yet Steve's actions had increased his suffering tenfold. The whole setup he'd created—taking someone's son or daughter and using and abusing their bodies for monetary gain—had ended in utter disaster.

More guests and family members came to Lavonia's aid, bringing buckets of water trying to extinguish her blazing body, but it was too late. It was too late to save her and too late to save the plan. Although I was devastated that Lavonia had taken her life, and in such a brutal way, I couldn't help but think my chances of escape had gone up in smoke, too. At least I was outside, in the free air...everyone was focused on Lavonia and Steve. Maybe, in a way, she had aided my escape. I still had an opportunity to flee.

The chaos deafening, I crept between trailers like a cat on the prowl, searching for Jenny. I snuck between cars, vans, anything I could hide behind. I caught sight of Olivia and her mum; they were watching events unfold through a window. I climbed up the three steps to their trailer, looked over my shoulder to check the coast was still clear, and slid open the bolt. The two women's mouths gaped wide. Before they could say anything, I implored them to move.

'Come on, it's time to go. We won't get another opportunity.'

'What about the others?' said Jenny.

'It's too risky. I'm not sure which trailers they're in. Let's just get out and alert the police.' I turned to step out of the door.

Jenny grabbed me by the shoulders and swung me round to face her. 'Take Olivia, I'll find the others.'

'Mum, it's too risky. You can't do this!' cried Olivia.

'I have to, I've been with them all from the start. I've witnessed their pain and, on occasion, added to their suffering. Plus, I can try and hinder anyone coming after you.'

I took a deep breath. 'We haven't got time for this. Let's go.'

Jenny gave us both a quick hug then smoothed her hair away from her face. 'I'm sorry, but if I can get the others, or even a van, I'll meet you at the top end of the common, near the motorway bridge. Go, now, head through the trees.'

Olivia tried pleading, but it was clear her mother had made her decision. 'Please, Mum, come on.'

'My priority is you,' Jenny said to her daughter, 'but I owe these girls. I love you, so go, before they know you're missing!'

Chapter Thirty-Nine

Obstacles

Olivia was devastated to leave without her mother in tow. I found it difficult to comprehend what was happening, I just focused on getting to the trees without incident or capture. Olivia's breath and frantic footsteps echoed behind me; we jogged at a fast pace. Screams and wails came from all directions; the gypsy clan tried to come to terms with Lavonia's death. The further we went, the more distant the sounds became.

I took in our surroundings, my heart racing, eyes on full alert. The dirt road led to an area dense with trees. The air was fresh and clean, and freedom was not far from our grasp. I glanced at Olivia and grabbed her hand; we set off like wild cougars, running as fast as we possibly could. Finally, we reached the safety of the woodland, our chests heaving, exhausted. We were hungry and dehydrated; adrenaline alone had willed us on.

'Which way?' asked Olivia.

I shrugged. 'I don't know, but I'm sure if we stick to the outskirts, we can still use the trees to hide. I don't fancy getting lost in the middle of there.'

We needed to catch our breath, so we walked in silence, my heart still racing. I couldn't stop thinking about Ben and Lavonia. It was almost as though Camp Hell was not a fitting enough title for such an evil place; it was more like Camp Death. And where the hell was John? Olivia kept peering behind us, in the direction of the campsite. I was sure she hoped to catch a glimpse of her mother. I was more concerned that someone would notice our absence. Before long, the camp was just a tiny speck on the horizon. I sighed; we weren't safe yet. Another obstacle faced us: marshland.

The area was dominated by grasses, reeds, and herbaceous plants, and flooded with large bodies of water. It was clear there had been some heavy rainfall and perhaps overspill from the rising river. The ground was waterlogged. It became harder to determine where to place our feet; we had to test the sodden earth with each step, to see if it would bear our weight. The wind picked up, and the air turned chilly. Our feet were soaking wet, the water above our ankles. Stepping stones helped us some of the way. Olivia yelled. Before I even turned to face her, I could tell she was hurt. Ironically, the stones that guided us also hindered us—she'd slipped on a huge stone covered in slimy moss.

'Sit for a moment,' I said. Her jeans were ripped at the knee, and blood oozed from the wound. 'Are you okay?'

'It's my ankle more than my knee.' She pulled up her jeans and grimaced. Already her ankle had ballooned with fluid.

'Do you think you can walk?' I panicked. What if she said no? I couldn't carry her.

Olivia wiped the blood from the open wound with the cuff of her cardigan. It was pretty deep. 'Yes, I think I'm fine.'

I hopped on one foot to take off one of my trainers then my soaking-wet sock. 'I know it's not a plaster or a bandage, but it may help for now.' I tied the sock around her knee in an attempt to stop the blood. 'There, that should do it.'

We both laughed. It was the first time I'd laughed since...well, I couldn't remember exactly when. The harsh wind whipped around us as a chilly reminder that we had to keep moving.

Although Olivia had said she was fine, the expression on her pale face didn't match her words.

'Let's go then,' I said, prompting her to move.

There was no way I wanted to be stuck there in the dark, the area was hard enough to navigate in the light. As she put weight onto her left foot, she winced. I threw my arm around her waist, and she used my shoulder as a crutch. Though she was tiny, I still felt her weight. Together, we struggled on.

Chapter Forty

No Escape

One of the abductees was caught, and there was a struggle. Jenny willed herself not to look in that direction, but she couldn't help it. Dave had the girl in his grasp, who screamed at the top of her lungs. She tried to stay on her feet. As nimble as she was, Dave had easily overpowered her with his strength. The other gypsy men were on the trail of the other escapees, sprinting towards them with their brows furrowed and a deadly determination to capture each and every one of them. Jenny's heart pounded; there was nothing she could do to assist them other than surrender herself, in the hope that one or more of them may get away.

She stood still and yelled, 'Run!'

She headed towards the girl struggling against Dave and tried to intervene. She suddenly stopped, fear immobilising her. The girl yelped, mimicking a helpless puppy. Dave tossed her to the ground; he kicked the child repeatedly in the head and didn't stop swinging his leg until the poor girl was still. Witnessing his final blow was as devastating to Jenny than if he'd been inflicting his wrath on her.

She gasped and set off towards the woodland. The sound of heavy boots on the ground became quicker, louder; within seconds, Dave was behind her. He grabbed Jenny's hair and pulled her clean off her feet. She froze at Dave's deadly glare and screamed so loudly her ears rang. She begged and pleaded, apologising over and over. He struck Jenny with such force that it knocked her to the ground. Her head thrummed, dizzy, as though she may fall asleep and never wake up.

'What the fuck are you playing at, bitch?' he spat.

'I'm sorry,' she managed to splutter. She trembled before him in the dirt.

Again, he dragged her to her feet. Jenny was deflated—the escape plan had been an epic failure. Most of the girls had been caught and were being escorted to the confines of the camp under heavy guard. It was obvious they would be severely punished.

The whole camp gathered together, as tight as a crowd at a concert, except this was no family show. The travellers watched the girls being marched through the centre of the camp, a walk of shame. Jenny could only think that, as they were the ones turning a blind eye, the shame was on them. Even though she was devastated at being captured, she was relieved and comforted that Olivia and Amber had broken out. Maybe they'd already called the authorities and the hostages would be saved after all?

Whispers amongst the crowd turned into an eerie silence, the mood sullen. The shock of Lavonia's death still lingered strong, yet there was also fear in the air. Steve came towards her; she could tell by his body language that he was ready to burst with raw grief and violent anger. Jenny knew how he thought, he would be working out who had to pay. Steve took hold of Jenny by the arm and forced her to stand in front of an old oak tree. She guessed she was the one to be made an example of—a lesson, a spectacle, for all to see. His status was still the uppermost thing in his mind.

The other girls were made to stand and watch. Jenny told herself: *Don't cry, hold your head up high.* She stared at them all one last time. The girls sobbed, but Jenny was glad that at least they'd tried. She knew what was coming before Steve even pulled the gun from his back pocket. He pointed the barrel at her, and it rested tight against her temple. She closed her eyes and thought of Olivia…her daughter's icy-blue eyes, golden locks, and her perfect body, as yet untouched by these bastards. She prayed in that moment, not for herself, but for her daughter's safe passage. She prayed that Olivia would enjoy a long, happy life, that she'd never be touched by evil and that she would embrace her freedom.

More pressure was applied to her temple. Her legs were weak, and her stomach churned. The bullet broke through her skin and ricocheted into her brain. Every nerve screamed in agony, then the light faded before her eyes until she was consumed by darkness.

Her body slumped to the ground. Onlookers screamed, petrified that they may be next in line.

Steve spat on Jenny's dead body. 'Where the hell is Olivia and Amber?' he snarled.

Not one of the girls found the courage to answer. He stomped forward and gripped one girl by the throat. He raised the gun. 'Open your mouth.'

The girl followed his instructions, tears welling, her body shaking.

He inserted the pistol into her mouth. 'Someone tell me now, where the fuck are they?'

'We honestly don't know. Jenny was by herself,' said one girl, panic in her voice.

'Try and escape again, and you're next. Remember, you're all disposable.' He eased the gun from the shaking girl's mouth and pointed it at each one of them as a warning.

He wasn't stupid, he needed these girls intact to keep the money flowing, but his authority had been challenged. He had to show them who was in charge. Compounded with his fiery temper was indescribable sorrowful grief that had come from watching his daughter burn to death.

Chapter Forty-One

Road to Freedom

By now, it was late afternoon. I'd managed to help Olivia hobble through the worst of the marshland, after stopping for several rest breaks—thankfully, the ground had become more manageable.

There wasn't a village or town in sight. A motorway loomed on the horizon, but we had a long way to go to reach it. Our pace slowed, and we battled through the brisk wind and a downpour. Our fingers were blue, and we were shivering; my throat was parched, and my legs ached, but I reminded myself that we'd got this far and we could cover the distance before nightfall.

Olivia complained of discomfort; she limped along. The pain in her ankle was gradually becoming worse.

I told her firmly, 'You need to master it. Grit your teeth. Think of how lucky we are to have escaped a different kind of pain.' I wasn't being very sympathetic, but she needed to be reminded of the suffering we'd left behind.

She sighed heavily. I couldn't go soft on her, I had to be her driving force.

The sun dropped behind the hills. The motorway wasn't far now.

'We can flag down a car or use the roadside assistance phone,' I told Olivia.

We clambered across the landscape; we were on the final stretch. Civilisation! I sighed, an instant relief. We'd escaped. We were going to survive. We smiled at each other, even though our legs were tired and weary.

Hunched over, we ascended the steep embankment before the motorway, gritted our teeth, sweat oozing from every pore. Olivia struggled. I turned to offer her a helping hand, then my jaw dropped. I instantly recognised the Transit speeding around the winding bend.

'Hurry!' I yelled, pulling on Olivia's arm.

Her eyes were wide with fear. We stopped climbing, alerted by the screech of tyres on gravel which brought the van to a dramatic halt. Before we could put our brains into gear, the passenger door swung open and Dave jumped out at the same time as Steve.

'Fuck! RUN!' I screamed.

My feet picked up pace. Olivia slipped on the damp grass, her injured ankle a real hindrance. My heart beat so hard that I thought it might explode. The brothers lunged forward. I ran as fast as my legs could carry me up the embankment. I couldn't help Olivia, and guilt lay heavily on me. I told myself to keep going…maybe I could save all of them, have these operations closed down and these two fuckers put behind bars. Olivia yelped. I looked over my shoulder; they'd already grabbed her. She screamed for help, her legs and arms flailing and kicking with the little energy she had left. They tossed her into the back of the Transit. I sprinted with every ounce of energy. The pair were unable to reach me before I threw my legs over the metal railings. I was sure I saw a gun in Steve's right hand; he aimed it in my general direction like I was target practice.

Lorries sped past at great speed. Commuters, shoppers…all going about their life with no idea of my dilemma. I waved my arms hysterically, trying to catch someone's attention. Time had frozen. Steve was scampering up the hill…I thought about stepping into the busy road and ending it all. Finally, a car driven by an elderly woman pulled up on the hard shoulder. Her features were wrinkled yet warm.

'Are you okay?' she asked with concern.

'Help! I need the police. I'm being chased.'

The woman looked over the barrier. She saw the van and the two men climbing the hill. She noticed that one had a gun. 'Oh my!' she gasped. 'Quick, get in.'

I jumped in the car, locked the door, and she sped off.

It took me a moment to get my shit together. The heating in the car was on full blast. Even though I let my body gather the warmth, a chill of anxiety ran cold. I wondered what was going to happen to Olivia. Tears streamed down my face like someone had opened floodgates. My sobs answered the elderly woman's questions.

Chapter Forty-Two

Cravings

Mentally, Crane had become unhinged. He couldn't think straight. He was filled with spontaneous thoughts but spent no time considering the outcomes. Over the last year, he'd inflicted unnecessary pain on himself. Where had that got him? Locked up in a run-down trailer full of filth. He couldn't help thinking about what he'd experienced prior to this: unspeakable cruelty inflicted by others that had left him a wreck of a man. What the hell was he thinking? Had the force, society, or his addiction not seen him suffer enough?

The caravan door slowly opened. A voice with an Irish twang said, 'We'll deal with you later.'

Crane climbed to his feet and watched the stranger stumble through the doorway and sit in the corner. The door was then slammed shut and locked, making them both prisoners. They glanced at each other. Crane was curious. Who was this girl? Why was she limping, and why was she so thin and gaunt? Should he speak to her or say nothing? The effects of the drugs were wearing off. He was uneasy and agitated, lines of white powder dominating his thoughts. His body cramped; Crane didn't know if it was part of the withdrawal process or the fact he'd been thrown about the back of a Transit like a washing machine on full spin. He craved a fix and he craved an escape.

Crane rambled for what seemed like hours rather than minutes, without making any sort of sense; eventually, he managed to switch off his mouth. The girl gave her name as Olivia when she finally got a word in. She rubbed her swollen ankle, and her jeans were torn at the knee. Her face was heavy with worry.

He listened to her talk, a distraction from the voice in his head. Olivia spoke with sadness: she told of her recapture, of her mother, and the rest of the abductees. With each sentence she seemed to direct her pent-up anger towards him. Crane understood that she was just frustrated about her circumstances. He needed to fill in the blanks, but he felt sorry for her. He didn't want to push her too far. By the looks of her, she'd been through enough.

Olivia told him how her mother had to turn tricks and prepare other hostages for a life in the slavery-sex-gang-racketeer trade. It was clear she blamed her mother for being so trusting and leading them both there in the first place. At the same time, she was worried about her. Suddenly, she jumped to her feet. She banged her fists repeatedly on the trailer walls. 'I want to see my mother, you bastards!'

'I tried that,' said Crane, holding up his bloody knuckles. 'Nobody came.'

Olivia slumped in a heap, her back against the wall. She sobbed. 'What if Amber hasn't escaped? What if she hasn't made it out and informed the police? What if they've locked her up, too?'

Crane's ears pricked up. 'Amber? As in Amber Hart?'

'Yes, why?' Olivia wiped the snot from her nose.

'She was a person of interest.'

'What do you mean?'

'A missing person. Someone I was investigating.'

'So, you're a copper and you ended up here? God help us all,' Olivia wailed, flinging her arms in the air.

Olivia's words stung. Another blow to Crane's already fragile ego. He was a copper…a copper who put his addiction and needs first. Christ, he chastised himself, sort your head out. He thought about it hard—it was all falling into place, his suspicions confirmed. Darren covered for the gypsies and their crimes. It wasn't just human slavery, it was sex trafficking, kidnapping, and a whole host of other things he'd not yet pieced together. But what was the point? He was a hostage himself, and he probably wasn't going to get out alive, which would add 'cop killer' to the gang's growing list of heinous crimes.

In that moment, he questioned whether he *wanted* to get out alive. Did he have the strength to be humiliated all over again by his peers and colleagues? Was it time to let the darkness inside fully consume him?

Chapter Forty-Three

At the Station

Momentarily frozen to the seat of the car, I gave my head a shake. I'd escaped but, as I sat outside the police station, I sobbed as though the whole world was crashing down on me.

Margaret, the old woman who had rescued me, had been ever so kind. She'd brought me to safety, but she couldn't hold my hand or tell my story. I had to do it on my own. I thanked her, thinking she would drive away, but she insisted on escorting me through the station's doors. I truly appreciated her kindness, something that had been decidedly lacking in my life. It took me several moments to gather my thoughts and emotions—to process what I had gone through, and to acknowledge the fact I'd finally reached safety.

The desk sergeant seemed more concerned with his coffee than my fragile state. I could feel a sensation trickle over me, the colour draining from my face. I was weak and exhausted. Margaret noticed my discomfort; she cupped her arm in mine as though to steady me.

She coughed loudly. 'This girl has been kidnapped and been put through hell. Kindly put the coffee down and do your job.'

The sergeant looked startled at her tone and classy accent, and probably sensed that this woman was no pushover.

Before long, I was in an interview room known as a comfort suite, not that there was much comfort: a couch, a desk and a chair, the walls brilliant white. I glugged cup after cup of water from the dispensary to quench my thirst, though I couldn't seem to quench the ache in my heart. I went over events whilst two officers listened. I wasn't sure if the interviewing officers took me seriously, their faces gave nothing away; after all, I was a foster kid who had fled to the streets. No one really gave a fuck about rogue kids in care.

The hours passed slowly, and after I'd named Jenny, Olivia, John Benson, and Ben Wilson, they seemed to take my allegations more seriously. One officer asked if I'd come across a Detective Crane, who had been on my 'missing person' case. I confirmed that I'd never seen or heard of someone with that name.

Sometime later, I was designated a female officer called Angela Parker, and again I had to repeat my account. The system grated on my nerves...there were people out there, slaves, who needed rescuing. I couldn't help but show my annoyance.

'Stop asking the same questions and go to the camp. Help them, rescue them. Arrest the gypsy bastards and do your job!'

The officers tried to offer words of reassurance.

'It's all in hand,' Angela said. 'I'm sorry the process isn't a nice one, but unfortunately, we need to gather every bit of evidence.'

I was then taken down the corridor. Specialists took photographs of me and swabbed for DNA. My clothes were put in a bag, and they gathered various samples from intimate and non-intimate parts of my body. I was violated all over again, as if being raped and beaten wasn't enough. In that room I felt like a sample in a science project; the whole process, clinical and as cold as ice, the officers documenting my sadness like it was an everyday occurrence. I wore shame and humiliation, my fragile body once again being moved and explored at someone else's behest.

Chapter Forty-Four

Raid

The campsite was under siege. National Crime Agency officer Carl Robinson led the investigation. Officers stood guard at the blue-and-white-taped cordon that surrounded the area, keeping reporters at bay. Speculation was rife, rumours were already doing the rounds.

From the outside, it looked like any other gypsy camp. To its victims, this had not been the case, and the site held sinister secrets. Robinson had been working undercover for some time; he'd accessed the club on several occasions, gathering as much intel as possible. He'd only recently learned that Darren had tipped the brothers off previously, which was why Robinson had never witnessed inappropriate behaviour. He was delighted that various forces were collaborating on the case—finally, these bastards could be brought to justice. The agencies had pooled their information with the Modern Slavery Human Trafficking Unit (MSHTU), whose field of expertise involved the exploitation of the vulnerable and forced labour. They, too, were already aware of Darren's involvement, they just needed evidence to support their findings.

Working together, the units searched Brenton Camp with a fine tooth-comb. They found the squalid, filthy living conditions in which the slaves had been forced to sleep and rest, a far cry from the perfectly clean trailers with mod cons the gypsy families inhabited. It was heartbreaking to think that these vulnerable people had been forced to work, with little food in their stomachs. The community turned a blind eye; they strolled around in designer clothes, with the latest iPhones and driving top-of-the-range cars. Were the gypsies afraid, soulless, or were they just corrupted by sheer greed?

Darren bowed his head in shame when he was handcuffed. He was paid to liaise between offices, keep tabs, maintain law and order, and report any kind of criminal activity; instead, his greed had tainted his judgment and got him into his predicament.

When the officers had swooped in, they didn't find it a smooth operation. They'd had to dodge stones, cans, and insults that were thrown their way. A group of gypsy guys, led by Lee, even threw punches. The gang swung baseball bats at the officers, too, and the rest of the community trembled in fear.

In total, seventeen arrests were made. Twenty-three victims were rescued—mostly teenage girls and one Detective Crane, who seemed agitated. He was more concerned with getting to the glove box of his vehicle than answering questions. Willow Farm also housed another five hostages of Chinese descent; the boys had been trafficked from abroad, and all were close to dying from starvation. The body of a Caucasian male was found hanging from the rafters of a barn.

It was clear to each arresting officer that, in one way or another, every victim had been broken. It was also clear, once the perpetrators were cuffed and taken away, that not all of the community agreed with the crimes that had taken place in the camp. They'd obviously felt intimidated and were too afraid to speak out for fear of retaliation. They were probably just as isolated as the slaves; after all, a gypsy king as wicked as Steve was a master at dehumanising folk. It was likely that the travellers feared being cast out by their own kind.

Jenny's body was found where she'd literally dropped, her twisted features for all to see. A burnt corpse of the Gypsy King's daughter, Lavonia, was discovered on a bed in a trailer; her mother lay next to her body, sobbing hysterically. In that same trailer was a gun, which was taken to the lab to confirm prints.

The search uncovered more information and evidence: a number of tenancy agreements for various houses in nearby villages, paperwork connected to further hostages—plus a whole host of documentation used to falsely claim benefits; numerous people's bank details and identity cards. There were other slaves holed up in properties in the surrounding area. Steve and his profiteering ring had been collecting the victims' money; it was common knowledge within the agency that slaves were escorted to job centres and benefit agencies. Under the watchful eyes of these crooks, many victims were exploited. The Gypsy King had a lot to answer for: abduction, holding everything belonging to an individual; controlling food, housing, money, work…it was all part and parcel of his wicked manipulation.

When I heard of his arrest, I wondered how he would cope in a cell—his choices taken away and his life controlled by prison guards. In a way, he was now a hostage…to the state.

Chapter Forty-Five

Realisation

Before I left the station, I needed some clarification for my own sake. The officers reassured me that it wasn't my stupidity that had led me to become a slave. The monsters preyed on the vulnerable, they manipulated people when they were at their lowest…the disabled, the needy, the lost. It was more common than the general public believed.

Slavery was apparently not something rife in a faraway country—it happened here, in the UK, on a daily basis.

They informed me that Ben's body had been recovered, as had Jenny's. It had hit me hard when Lavonia told me of his hanging, but back then I had to concentrate on saving myself. I recalled the first time I'd encountered him, shackled, in the barn. His innocence, his stammer, his strange view of the world…he didn't deserve such a cruel ending to his life. The only way I could justify his death in my head was believing that he was finally at peace, that his suffering had ended.

With regards to Jenny, the devastating truth was that she'd sacrificed herself and her future with her daughter to help others escape. She did have a heart after all, she just didn't wear it for everyone to see. It took me several moments to gather my thoughts, to process the fact she was gone. I couldn't believe those brutes had murdered her with a single bullet to the head. The first time I'd encountered Jenny, her bosom bulging out of her basque, and in her trademark fishnet tights, I thought she was as hard as nails, but beneath that exterior was a woman who'd been broken, someone who'd been moulded to do the Gypsy King's bidding without complaint.

I hadn't seen Olivia yet; apparently, a doctor was tending to her ankle. I was relieved she'd been found safe.

So many names were thrown at me that day that my head swirled. I didn't recognise most of them, though some were familiar. I heard that the detective who had been searching for me had also been held against his will at the camp, which made me realise just how dangerous these people were. It put things into perspective; things were a whole lot bigger than I'd imagined. I was curious as to how the others had suffered at the hands of the perpetrators; at the same time, I wasn't sure my fragile state of mind could handle any more horror.

To my disappointment, John had not been located. I felt in my bones that he'd come to some sort of devastating end. Even though I wasn't religious, I needed to honour him and pray for his soul. In the early days of my torment, when my stomach had grumbled and my throat was closing over through thirst, he'd shared his sandwich, even though his own body was fragile, weak, and malnourished. It was such a selfless act, and one I'd never forget.

My head spun, crammed to the brink with information overload. I craved the simple things most people take for granted: a hot bath, and a comfy bed with crisp, clean sheets. Although a PC had given me a portion of cheesy chips, which I'd greedily devoured in a matter of moments, I was still hungry. Having so little food for so long was the reason it was constantly in my thoughts.

I wasn't sure where I was going to stay that night or the night to follow. I'd been assigned a case worker whose job it was to get me through the final steps before court. The realisation hit me that this wasn't over. I'd have to tell my story yet again. All I wanted to do was put it to bed. I never wanted to think of Camp Hell for another second. I had to wipe the memories clean.

Chapter Forty-Six

Humiliation

Crane was humiliated as he stepped into the station. All eyes were on him. He was paranoid and irritated that he hadn't got results. Already the hum of whispers swirled around him, throughout the whole station. He looked a mess. His suit was stained from sitting in that filthy trailer, and his body clammy, which reflected the mess going on inside him. He was annoyed with the world, but mostly, with himself.

As he headed to the sergeant's office, he passed Robinson. The agent paused, his hands on his hips.

He said to Crane, 'Close, mate. You nearly got yourself killed there.'

Crane didn't like Robinson's sarcastic tone or his stance. He squeezed his knuckles until they turned white. He wanted to land a right hook on Robinson's smug face, but instead, he kept his temper at bay and held himself together. He simply nodded at the agent and continued down the corridor.

After knocking on the sergeant's door, he smoothed down his suit in a bid to iron out the creases. He waited patiently until the sergeant shouted 'Enter'. As soon as he stepped in front of his superior, his stomach twisted. He'd been here before. A black mist of bad memories resurfaced as his previous assault crawled to the forefront of his mind. He'd wanted to numb those memories, yet he'd stupidly followed the same dangerous path.

Sergeant Cole sat in a chair in front of the window. The room was claustrophobic and humid, even though a fan blew out cold air. He watched the breeze gently ruffle the sergeant's hair, revealing a bald spot, central on his head. Given the bucket full of gel the sergeant used each day, it was clear he desperately wanted to disguise it.

'Detective Crane, do you need a doctor?'

'No, I'm fine,' Crane grunted. He'd self-medicated before coming to the station, inhaling the familiar white powder up his nose and rubbing it along his gums whilst he sat in his car.

'Clearly, you're not fine. I seem to think that, since your last accident, you're not following protocol. You didn't leave a log or inform anyone that you were about to tackle something this big on your own.'

'I didn't realise, Sarge, that it was 'this big'.' Crane shrugged.

'What the hell were you thinking?'

'I was just following a lead.'

'A lead you thought you could handle yourself. I think we've been here before, haven't we?' the sergeant chastised.

Crane stood upright, but inside he was crushed small. He didn't have the energy or inclination to talk back; all he could think about was numbing the pain, a pain that was so very deep. His thoughts and feelings were so dark, he needed them whipped and beaten from his mind, body, and soul.

'I'm sorry, Detective, but I feel you're in no fit state to work. You've been a bloody idiot. I think you need some leave again—your irrational thinking put you in danger. It could also have affected the other agencies' investigations.'

Crane didn't argue. What was the point? He'd fucked up time and time again. He reached into his pocket, pulled out his ID, and dropped it on the desk. Without a word, he turned on his heel and left the room. The sergeant's office vibrated from the force of the door being slammed shut.

Chapter Forty-Seven

The Hostel

I was temporarily placed in the Beverley Hostel. The air
reeked of cannabis, sweat, and alcohol. The narrow
corridors had woodchip on the walls, dirty windows, and
stained carpets. My case worker escorted me to a tiny room
with one small window, a single bed, and a tatty chest of
drawers. Still, it was a step up from the rusty caravan, though
I couldn't help but compare it to the home comforts Steve and

his family had enjoyed in the lavish farmhouse at Willow Farm. It disgusted me how he'd obtained it, by profiteering off the vulnerable. From weak, lonely people, just like me. I hoped prison would hold the brothers for a very long time; I considered that even a prison cell would have more luxuries than this halfway house. This particular shelter harboured the unwanted and forgotten. I was already familiar with those feelings.

I glanced around the place and considered my circumstances. I felt that, yet again, I'd been wronged. Stuck in a hellhole with hookers, druggies, and alcoholics—was my life not worth more? It was as if I had to endure one punishment after another. This wasn't living, it was merely existing. I had no hope, no plans for the future. All I could look forward to was becoming another government statistic drawing benefits. The numerous counselling sessions I'd need to attend, to deal with my baggage. The whole thing stank, I'd been doomed from the start. Where was my guardian angel? The more I pondered, rage spewed from every nerve ending. Prison was too good for Steve and Dave. They deserved much more…pain, castration, even death.

I glared at the four walls, trying to take my mind off the first day of the trial, even though it was weeks away. Wallpaper drooped in the corners, and black mould grew behind it. I felt just as torn, shabby, and drab in comparison. I shivered from memories and the icy temperature, my mind a mass of despair and confusion. I didn't believe that the court case would fully draw a line under the torture I'd endured, though my counsellor said it was a good place to start. What the hell did she know? I saw her walk back to her BMW; with her Louis Vuitton pumps and painted fingernails, it was clear she'd never suffered a day of hardship during her entire life.

214

I stared out of the window. It wasn't a pretty view. I was faced with towering red brick walls, which were indicative of my mood and state of mind. I was physically and mentally exhausted. I'd found it hard to sleep the previous night, my nightmares wouldn't leave me, and the trial constantly circulated through my thoughts. Neither could I rid my mind of the image of Steve's twisted face and the pain he put me through...the moment he thrust himself upon me, his smirk and cruel words. And I would never forget the sheer hunger I'd endured.

I asked myself if I had the strength to face him in court, to face any of the gypsy clan. Did I have enough faith in the British justice system? What about the media?

I couldn't remember if I'd even slept at all. I'd watched the hand of the wall clock tick every minute and I'd counted every hour. I was numb—I didn't want to stand before any of them, their faces haunted me enough already. Before long it was 8 a.m. I dragged my feet to the shared bathroom. Strangers lined the corridor, but I wouldn't make eye contact or speak. I must have worn my shame like a beacon for all to see. Eventually, I splashed my face with cold water. A sickness surged in my gut. I became lightheaded, confused. My anguish weighed as heavy as lead. I glared at the girl in the mirror. Dark circles sat under her eyes, and her skin appeared pale and sickly. I shook my head and gave myself a pep talk. *You can do this. You can't let them win.* The sickness quickly accumulated into a rapid churning and twisting in the pit of my stomach, growing into anger and hate, which willed me on.

I later met with my counsellor. I didn't do much talking, I just listened. I didn't want to talk about my ordeal. I wanted to squash it, put it away.

Chapter Forty-Eight

Numb

Days later, Crane lay naked on the bed. Clara, in her tight basque, her voluptuous breasts on the verge of escaping, she seemed to be the only person who understood him. It wasn't spoken, yet there was a bond with her, an emotional trust and a connection that would never be questioned. The studded paddle stung the flesh of his back and buttocks. Lately, he'd been consumed by his depression and become obsessed with finding that peak, the adrenaline, the endorphins, that made him feel alive. He had to mask the humiliation somehow. He'd upped his sessions from once a week to daily; in fact, his usual hour-long appointment was now a marathon session of controlled spankings for more than two hours a day, until his body was raw. It was the only time he didn't feel burdened; with each strike his worries diminished. His drug use had also increased, and it threatened to spiral out of control. His employment status was also out of his hands.

His need for Clara's punishment was not borne from a love of all things kinky—it was about control. With each blow of the paddle, he tested whether he could withstand the pain; if not, he was free to walk away at any moment. As the studs punctured his skin, the pain made him aware that, although he felt numb, he wasn't dead yet.

Clara hit him with a final blow. She knew Crane's body well by now and recognised its shift from tense, stiff and rigid, to a state of relaxation. A state in which he could think clearly, assess his choices. He wondered how he could have done things differently, how he could have been the hero rather than the jester.

His mind pored over the case's recent activity. In a flash, he realised that John Benson's body had never been retrieved. Where was his body; was he still alive? Was it worth looking into? Crane was still on gardening leave, yet he didn't have anything else to do. He could snoop around, maybe clear his name and change how others saw him…go from loser to winner. It was worth a chance, wasn't it?

Crane didn't foresee such a result when he'd woken that morning. Maybe Clara had beaten some sense into him, or perhaps it was his messed-up, drug-infested mind. He left her premises, leaving his cash on the table, and walked towards his car. He ordered a takeaway coffee from the Starbucks' drive-thru and took a sip before setting it in the holder—that was when he realised he was already on the way to Willow Farm. He had a hunch, and it was worth a shot.

Clara had told him, 'Do what feels right, follow your gut.' And that's exactly what he did.

Chapter Forty-Nine

A Visitor

Another crazy night in the halfway house. It wasn't just the comings and goings of other guests that stopped me from sleeping. Hours had passed, and I hadn't slept a wink. I began to think that I may die of hyperthermia; the room was Baltic-cold.

My nightmares were terrifying. I sat up in bed, the duvet wrapped tightly around me for warmth and comfort. I was exhausted and anxious; my memories would not let me rest. My head crammed with unanswered questions and horrors that wouldn't still. Fear of the court case, fear of the process, and fear over the sentence the monsters would receive, played on my mind.

There was an erratic thumping at the door. Panic ran through me like an electric shock. Was it one of the gypsy gang intent on retribution? Was I in danger? It had never crossed my mind until that point. I pulled the duvet over my head, wishing for whoever it was to go away. Then a familiar voice, "Hello, its Olivia."

I leapt from the bed, dropping the duvet, and rushed to open the door. Olivia stood there, her long golden locks scraped back into a tight ponytail. Her blue eyes brimmed with tears.

'I hope you don't mind me showing up. I had to see you.'

I threw my arms around her and held her close. 'I'm so happy you're safe.'

We both sobbed, recalling our horrific events and sharing tears of freedom. There were no words that could have comforted her pain...our pain...all we could do was be there for one another. It was strange to be together without being under lock and key.

She'd come to tell me the news about her mother. I didn't tell her that I already knew of Jenny's death. I let Olivia talk about it and process her feelings; she was devastated, and her words were heartbreaking.

'I've thought of nothing but freedom for years. I've cried to be set free, but now my mother's gone, I'm lost and alone. I have nothing left in the world.'

Feeling lost and alone was familiar to me, never having had a family to tend to my needs, and being in the care system made me feel that way. 'We have each other. I'll always be here for you, no matter what. Your mum was a hero, you have to hold on to that. Without her, none of us would have escaped. She put her life on the line. She gave us a fighting chance, and now we're all free.'

'Are we really free?' she asked. 'I've had newspaper reporters following me, watching my every step. They've printed things in the paper about my mother, referring to her as a single mother on benefits, hooked by traffickers. Everywhere I turn, I can't flee from it. I feel like I'm literally going out of my mind.'

I held her hand, looked into her eyes, and told her firmly, 'The media is a goddamn evil. You know what reporters are like…next week, it'll be someone or something else. All we can do is stay strong, and once the court hearing is out of the way, I'm sure we can put it behind us…start afresh. We'll be fine.'

I wasn't sure if I was trying to convince Olivia or myself. The truth was, we'd never be fine, the damage had been done. There would be no forgetting the pain, the torment, it ran too deep. I didn't want to tell her that I hadn't slept for days, that I could smell the perverts on my skin, still feel the sting of brutal beatings and an emptiness in my stomach. All I could do was try to convince her, for the sake of her mental health.

Chapter Fifty

Taking a Risk

Crane sped down the motorway. He couldn't stop thinking about the guy who had not been recovered, John Benson. It was a hunch, and although his previous spontaneous actions had resulted in disaster, he still followed his gut. He felt that, no matter how twisted a mind was, no individual or group of individuals would dump a body on a campsite so close to family, friends, and prying eyes. Not if they had loads of land at their disposal on a property named Willow Farm.

He questioned whether he was overthinking things—were his conclusions a result of the lines of coke he'd inhaled? Were his thoughts distorted? Should he spin the vehicle round and drive home? The case didn't really concern him anymore, he'd already turned in his ID. He told himself that, at least if he could solve this tiny twist in the tale, it was something. He had to earn respect somehow.

Yellow tape still lined the perimeter of the farm. A sign stated that the home was subject to a repossession order—as it had been bought with dirty cash it was an asset under the Proceeds of Crime Act. That the home was abandoned would benefit him greatly, he thought. It would give him time to snoop around undisturbed. Maybe he would come to a dead end and find nothing, but it was a hunch worth following.

He pulled on his jacket, taking in the scenic location. It was a beautiful landscape. He walked for miles until his feet hurt, searching for any scrap of evidence. There seemed to be endless green fields; surely, he surmised, if you were going to dump a body, you couldn't carry it this far. It would be a dead weight and would need to be transported by vehicle. A patch of grassy land looked like it had been driven over. The tracks weren't wide enough to have come from a tractor—a car or van, maybe. He stuck to the track and found they led to the land's boundary. Crane scratched his head. He was confused as to why the tracks led to a fence that had no gateway or access beyond.

He picked up his pace and combed the boundary, and that's when he discovered an uneven mass of dirt. It was clear the mound had been recently dug and smoothed over. Goddamn it. He cursed himself for not bringing a shovel. He dropped to his knees and began removing topsoil with his hands. It wasn't an easy task, but he kept at it.

After some time, he touched something; it felt like plastic. He tugged at it with all his strength, until the earth moved. He gasped. Protruding from the dirt, wrapped in plastic, was a human hand.

He fumbled in his jacket pocket for his mobile. 'Sarge, you've got to get down to Willow Farm. I've found a body.'

'What do you mean? Are you nuts? You're on leave.'

'I followed a hunch, and I've found a dead body.'

The sergeant sighed. 'Goddamn it, Crane, this isn't authorised. We're going to have to tweak the paperwork.'

Before long, a whole team had arrived. They exhumed not just John Benson's body, but a mass grave of unknown victims, male and female. Each one had been buried in plastic or hessian sacks. It was a huge result for Crane. In total, seven corpses were unearthed, all at different stages of decomposition.

That afternoon, Crane walked from the scene with his head held high. He'd uncovered something that no one else had even considered looking for, something that added a great deal of weight to the case. For the first time in a long time, he didn't feel numb, he felt like he'd accomplished something. He wasn't quite the failure others tended to see. Whilst on a high note, he decided it was time to hang up his ID for good.

Chapter Fifty-One

Verdict

The courtroom was packed tightly with both men and women from the gypsy community—they made up an obstreperous crowd that had obviously come to show support for the accused. The prosecutor sat at a table immediately in front of the bench, on the judge's right side. The jury listened to the evidence relating to each victim. Craig Lowe from the media was there to report the case.

The prosecutor addressed the judge before speaking to the court. The evidence was substantial, he said, as he summarised the horrific conditions and experiences the slaves had encountered. Living in squalor, the now-deceased John Benson had been a hostage for as long as thirteen years, before his life was cruelly taken from him and his body dumped in a shallow grave.

The prosecutor spoke with disgust, emphasising the humiliation the victims endured. 'Whilst these slaves were degraded and forced to live like pigs, the accused roamed free and built an empire. Some may say the nomadic lifestyle is simply different from our own, yet this duo owned mobile homes on Brenton Camp—informally known as Camp Hell—as well as on surrounding campsites and residences, which were all occupied by their human cargo.

'Both of the accused were the ringleaders. They had others following their orders, which added to the individuals' misery. Each member of this gang wilfully exploited both men and women between the ages of fifteen to sixty-two for monetary gain. The wealth from their ill-gotten gains allowed them to buy land and lavish homes for their offspring and spouses to live in. They profited from illegal schemes whilst their hostages were forced to live in cramped, foetid conditions with minimal resources. They were worked and treated like dogs, with no money and little food for reward. The caravans were essentially metal prisons without water or heating. Men were forced to spend their days labouring as ground workers, under a keen eye, whilst the female and disabled slaves were ordered to cook and clean. Girls as young as fifteen were involuntarily coerced into sexual slavery and pressurised to lie with paying punters every night of the week.'

The barrister went on, and the majority of those in court found the details difficult to stomach. The jury heard that beatings were a regular thing, that some hostages were plied with drugs, cigarettes, and booze, which further enabled the cruel clan to have complete control over them. Some victims hadn't cashed their benefits for years; instead, the brothers had accessed their bank accounts and stolen their money and their identities from them.

The pair's defence team attempted to argue that food and accommodation was adequate payment for their 'workers'. The appalling truth was that there was a much bigger price paid, concerning their victims' mental and physical health. The slaves who survived had clarified in their statements that, often, they were restricted to the families' leftovers, and that, on occasion, they were even forced to eat dog food for the gang's amusement.

Lee Murphy and his cronies were convicted of Ben Wilson's murder and sentenced to life. The list of misdemeanours was lengthy for every person brought into the dock. The cannabis factory running from Steve Murphy's property was added to the accused's rap sheets, as were the murders of the seven bodies unearthed by Detective Crane. The victims had recently been identified; all were classed as vulnerable and on the missing person's list.

The jury concluded that Steven and David Murphy had used extreme violence and extortion for personal gain. They would never be freed, each receiving whole life orders from the judge.

Chapter Fifty-Two

Distractions

Crane's state of mind was all over the place and of his own doing. His need for pain and control and a route to oblivion proved a significant distraction from his job. Now, he'd finally fulfilled his professional expectations. He didn't revel in his success, as it has arisen from the brutal deaths of several innocent people, and he accepted that his policing had suffered prior to this result. Things had to change. His decision not to return to the force brought relief. He was tired of feeling disappointed about his work— discovering those bodies at Willow Farm meant he could leave on a high.

He recognised that the high wouldn't last. It wouldn't be long until he sank to rock bottom again. His services to the force hadn't always been acceptable to his peers, and his methods were largely unauthorised, which only brought trouble. He didn't have the stomach or the energy to continue.

Crane mulled over his years in service and questioned if he'd ever been a good copper—was it just that video of his beating going viral that had tipped him over the edge? He truly believed that if he hadn't endured that particular assault, he would never have followed his dark path towards pain and punishment. He was thankful to one person who never judged his weird ways—Clara—not just because she gave his body a good spanking and inflicted pain at his request, but because she gave him a chance to reach a state of peace. She helped him cope with his habits and actions, which were often unhealthy and carried a risk. Every line he snorted, someone could have died under his watch; every time he'd been wasted and got behind the wheel of a vehicle, someone could have been killed. Allowing drugs to control his thoughts gave him a dangerous sense of invincibility, which could have seen a gypsy gang snuff out his life as easily as extinguishing a candle.

At Crane's next appointment with Clara, she encouraged him to get help with his cocaine addiction. She offered to be his sponsor, to feel his pain, whether that meant talking it out or tackling it with a paddle in hand—whatever it required. She didn't hold back and told him straight, 'You've lost yourself. You're slipping deeper into a depression, and the drugs are just masking your issues.'

Crane admitted she was right; he couldn't go on like this, meeting dealers in dark alleys. He had to embrace his pain, take charge of his emotions.

The very next day, he arranged an appointment with his GP. He was determined to kick the drug habit, but he wasn't prepared to give up Clara. He always thought the two vices went hand in hand, but a part of him didn't want to let her go. Crane needed someone stern, forceful…someone who made him feel alive. That someone was Clara.

Chapter Fifty-Three

Justice

I used to struggle to understand what made people kill, except, perhaps, psychopaths featured in books and on TV. Now, though, after surviving such awful circumstances, I could see how one could be motivated to hurt the person or persons who had hurt you.

Lately, I'd thought of nothing else. I was consumed by hate, devoured by a darkness that swallowed me up. I was haunted by horrific memories, disturbed by what I saw, what I did…I thought of all the places I'd been taken to against my will, all the wicked deeds that were forced upon me. I'd processed the pain, yet it still lingered.

I wondered what other people would have done in the same situation. Would they have become similarly consumed? Would they have shrivelled up and hidden away? Or would they have doused the burning in their soul by getting their revenge? One word kept circulating in my thoughts: neglect. Neglect was a familiar word to me—I'd been neglected by my drug addict of a mother, neglected by the system, neglected by man's cruel hand. The damage was done, I'd been contaminated by hate and man's dirty seed. I yearned to feel cleansed. I wanted to be rid of the stench of sin on my skin. I wanted to erase the torment. All I could think about was my pain, my suffering; I doubted the affliction of my distress would ever leave me.

I came to a startling conclusion. It was a sign, I was being guided by a light, in the dark. There was a possibility that I could be cleansed. Have a clean body, a clear mind, a clear conscience.

I didn't want to become a wreck. I would never let my barriers down again, sorrow and sadness ran too deep. My scars were both mental and physical. I'd learnt a hard lesson ever since I was born: we're all in preparation for one thing only—to be alone. We grow up to simply become a statistic, working our fingers to the bone for someone else—a gang, the government, our family. No one has our back. No one cares. Everything we do, we must do it ourselves. We have no alternative but to embrace the fire in our bellies and the will to continue if we wish to survive in this cruel world. I was saddened, not just because of my encounter with Camp

Hell, I also identified that I had been let down by a self-absorbed society. Adrenaline pushed me to another level. I would not be defeated. I would not wither or crumble.

I chose to sit in a particular seat in the courthouse as Steve was sentenced. Regardless of what the court decided, I had to follow my own justice. He had taken something from me that could never be replaced: my virginity. This was his fault, he'd moulded me this way. The session over, I grasped the blade between my fingers. My feet sped towards him as he was escorted up the stairs, my eyes on nothing else. With every step my emotions accelerated into a blind rage. Full of loathing, I was untouchable.

It happened in the blink of an eye. Steve collapsed to the floor, clutching his throat. Blood seeped between his fingers and soaked into his white shirt and blue tie. In that moment, I smiled, exhilarated. Fear shone in his eyes, and I drank in the shock and the pain he displayed on his face. I'd obliterated the smug look the bastard usually wore, the one I saw in my nightmares when reliving the moments when he'd taken everything from me.

There was a brief silence followed by sheer panic. I could feel the commotion yet I remained calm. The guards grabbed me, but I wasn't fazed. Maria screamed at me; I couldn't take in what she was ranting about, my emotions were too heightened for me to listen. Instead, I grinned at her and waved the bloody blade in the air before the guards forced it from my grasp. I was buzzing with adrenaline.

Some people would argue that I was disturbed...mentally unhinged. I couldn't have cared less. I stood there like a wild, feral child, Steve's blood staining my palms, and all I felt was a sense of accomplishment. I couldn't walk away—what was the point? I had nowhere to go.

Though there was chaos all around me, I focused on Olivia in the crowd. I'd done this not just for myself, but for her, for her mother, for Ben, for John, and everyone else who'd suffered under that bastard 'Gypsy King's' hand. A shiver ran down my spine, which reminded me that I was alive and as free as I'd always wanted to be. A freedom of sorts...it had been my choice to annihilate him, and for the entire world to see his pain. Screams from Steve's family became louder as his life slipped away on the cold concrete steps. Their trauma, their suffering...it was music to my ears.

I was taken out of the building. The sun warmed my face, and I smiled. I knew I'd have to go to prison, but I guessed it couldn't be worse than some of the places I'd stayed. The difference being, I'd have my own room, running water, a bathroom, three meals a day, maybe even a PlayStation. I'd have access to books and the chance of an education. Perhaps I'd find a family—other broken souls who could relate to my loneliness, my anger and frustration at this godforsaken world.

A female officer stood before me, with more officers a few feet behind her. Her voice was calm and soft, 'Amber, put your head down and get in the car.'

I did as she'd asked, I had no beef with her. I couldn't even recall being cuffed; I must have accepted my arrest without resistance. The officer put her hand on my head and guided me into the back of the police car. I disappeared from the gathering crowd, many of whom were raging and throwing taunts and insults. I stared out of the window. My mind was ticking like a time bomb; I thought about my actions, about how I'd served my own justice. The law was a joke...where was justice when I was ripped from my mother's arms and thrown into care? Where was justice when my carer was all hugs and smiles in front of social workers, only to beat me or ignore me the minute the officials left?

News reports often feature cases where a judge has to take into account mitigating circumstances when sentencing. A rapist of a minor can serve just ten months, because of a corrupt system that protects the instigator rather than the victim—the same system that can order a chronically ill grandmother recovering from a broken hip to spend ten days in prison for non-payment of her TV licence. The law doesn't balance the scales of justice, it just lines the pockets of lawyers. I had no faith in law and order. I wasn't prepared to take that chance.

Was I wrong to apply my own justice? Would others have done the same if it had been their daughter, son, sister, brother? Wouldn't anyone want justice if they'd been failed by the system...kidnapped, raped, beaten? I believed that we should still have capital punishment—especially for horrific cases of murder, paedophilia, and slavery. The ultimate deterrent in a fake society. A world where everyone battled to shout the loudest...the keyboard warriors, the haters, the racists, the do-gooders. Morals...humbug. The system screwed me over from being a child. I took the decision to rid the earth of Steve. He'd taken something from me that had crushed me beyond repair—my innocence. It was inevitable that my mask would fall and the gloves would come off; society and my experiences had made me this way. For the first time in a long time, I was euphoric. I'd brought down the evil gang, ridding them of their leader for all eternity, and it felt good.

I didn't know it, but through each step of my trauma, I'd gained strength. I had what it took to survive. I'd crawled through the depths of Hell, picked up my shattered body and

241

crushed soul, and put them together again. The trauma, the horror, the torment I'd endured, would haunt me forever—my scars ran deep. The prison bars physically contained me, but I hardly noticed them. For the first time in my life, I felt free.

About the Author

Cheryl Elaine was born in Germany but moved to Northern Ireland as a young child. She then moved to Yorkshire, where she spent most of her childhood, and this is where she currently resides with her husband and three daughters.

Cheryl Elaine is an avid reader who also enjoys watching horror movies—the more gruesome, the better! She enjoys travelling and socialising but also loves spending time at home with her family and her ever-expanding menagerie, which currently includes two dogs, a budgie, seven pond fish, and sadly, Rocky the rat passed away.

If you enjoyed the book, please leave a review!